MAR 1989

/ 495

M
Sim

Simenon, Georges, 1903-
   Maigret on the Riviera / Georges
Simenon ; translated by Geoffrey
Sainsbury. -- 1st ed. -- San Diego :
Harcourt Brace Jovanovich, c1968.
   137 p. ; 22 cm.
   Translation of: Liberty bar.
   ISBN 0-15-155149-9

yellow stains 905 An

     I. Title

22 MAR 89   16832845   RSVAme   87-26866

Maigret on the Riviera

GEORGES SIMENON

Maigret on the Riviera

TRANSLATED BY
GEOFFREY SAINSBURY

A Helen and Kurt Wolff Book
Harcourt Brace Jovanovich, Publishers
San Diego   New York   London

Library of Congress Cataloging-in-Publication Data

Simenon, Georges, 1903–
  [Liberty bar. English]
  Maigret on the Riviera/by Georges Simenon; translated by
Geoffrey Sainsbury.
    p. cm.
  Translation of: Liberty bar.
  "A Helen and Kurt Wolff book."
  ISBN 0-15-155149-9
  I. Title.
PQ2637.I53L513   1988   87-26866
843'.912–dc19

Designed by Kaelin Chappell
Printed in the United States of America
First edition
A B C D E

Maigret on the Riviera

CHAPTER ONE

The Dead Man and His Two Women

It began with the feeling one has at the beginning of a vacation. When Maigret got off the train at Antibes, half the station was bathed in a blaze of sunlight, through which people moved like shadows—shadows in straw hats and white trousers, with tennis rackets in their hands. Spring had burst out suddenly, and the air hummed with the heat. On the other side of the platform were cactuses and palm trees and, farther off, a strip of blue sea.

Someone dashed up to him.

"Superintendent Maigret? I recognized you at once from a photograph in the papers. I'm Inspector Boutigues."

Boutigues. What a name.

The young inspector had already relieved Maigret of his luggage and was leading him toward the exit. He wore a pearl-gray suit and boots with half-cloth uppers; he had a red carnation in his buttonhole.

"Is this your first visit to Antibes?"

Maigret mopped his forehead and tried to keep up with his guide, who threaded his way nimbly through the crowd. Finally, they climbed into a cab—not a taxi, but a good old-fashioned fiacre, with a cream-colored top fringed by little tassels.

The dandling of the springs, the crack of the driver's whip, the dull sound of the horse's hoofs on the hot, soft asphalt brought back a long-forgotten sensation.

"We'll have a drink first. . . . Oh, yes! After a journey like that . . . Driver! Stop at the Café Glacier, will you?"

The Café Glacier was right around the corner.

"The center of Antibes," the inspector explained.

It was a charming square, with a garden in the middle, cream- or orange-colored awnings on every building. Under one of them, on the terrace of the café, the two men sat down and sipped anisette. Opposite was a shop window filled with bathing outfits, beach robes, and other such articles; on their left, a window full of cameras. Beautiful cars were parked along the curb.

Yes, it was more like a vacation than . . .

"Would you rather see the prisoners first or the house where he was killed?"

"The house," answered Maigret, hardly more conscious of what he was saying than if Boutigues had asked him "How are you?"

The vacation feeling continued. Maigret smoked the cigar Boutigues had offered him. The horse trotted along the road by the seashore. To the right were villas hidden among pine trees; to the left, rocks, then the expanse of blue sea uninterrupted except for two or three white sails.

"Shall I tell you where we are? We've left Antibes behind us, and from here on it's Cap d'Antibes. Nothing but villas, most of them pretty grand."

Maigret, blissful, was ready to accept anything that was said. His head seemed to be full of sunshine. His companion's carnation made him blink.

"Boutigues, you said?"

"Yes. I come from Nice. . . . A Niçois, or, rather, a Nicéen!"

In other words, the real thing—a Niçois to his fingertips, to the marrow of his bones.

"Lean over this way a little. You see that white house? That's it."

Maigret wasn't taking it seriously; he couldn't bring himself to believe that he was on a job, that he was here because somebody had been killed.

True, his instructions had been somewhat unusual:

"A man named Brown was murdered at Cap d'Antibes. The newspapers are blowing it up. It's a case that needs tactful handling and no trouble."

Understood.

During the war, Brown had worked for French intelligence, the Deuxième Bureau.

Doubly understood.

So here he was, with his head full of sunshine, having traveled almost six hundred miles to be tactful. The fiacre stopped. Boutigues took a key from his pocket, opened a gate, and led the way up a gravel path.

"This is one of the poorest villas on the Cap."

Even so, it wasn't bad. The air was heavy with the sweet smell of mimosa. Small orange trees still bore a few oranges. There were some queer-shaped flowers that Maigret had never seen before.

"The place across the way belongs to a maharajah. He's probably here now. . . . Farther along on the left is a famous writer, a member of the French Academy. And beyond him is a ballet dancer who lives with an English lord."

Yes! But what Maigret wanted more than anything was to sit down on the bench by the house and have a nap. After all, he'd been traveling the whole of the previous night.

"I'd better explain the household first."

Boutigues had opened the door, and they were standing in a cool room with windows looking out on the sea.

"Brown lived here for at least ten years."

"What did he do?"

"Nothing. He must have had private means. . . . Lived here with two women. 'Brown and his two women': that's how people spoke of them."

"Two?"

"Only one was his mistress: Gina Martini."

"Has she been arrested?"

"Yes. Her mother, too . . . The three of them lived here without a servant."

The house had certainly not been kept any too well. There were a few beautiful things in it, perhaps, a few pieces of good furniture, and here and there some objects that had had a moment of splendor. But everything was dirty, and the good things and the bad were jumbled together indiscriminately. There were too many carpets, antimacassars, and hangings; too many dust collectors.

"Now, here are the facts. There's a garage next to the house, where Brown used to keep his old-fashioned car. He used it mostly for shopping in Antibes."

"Yes," sighed Maigret, who was watching a man with a split reed fishing in the clear water for the sea urchins that lay on the bottom.

4

"For three days, however, the car was left standing in front of the house. People noticed, but nobody bothered about it. It was nobody's business. . . . And it wasn't till Monday evening—"

"Just a moment. It's Thursday now, isn't it? . . . Go on."

"On Monday evening, a butcher was driving back to Antibes in his van. He saw the old car start—you can read his statement. As he came up behind it, he thought Brown must be drunk. The car was lurching forward. Then it went along steadily for a while. But at the first bend, it crashed into the rock at the side of the road.

"The butcher stopped, but before he could do anything, two women got out of the car and started running."

"Were they carrying anything?"

"Three suitcases . . . It was getting dark. The butcher didn't know what to do. Finally, he simply drove past the women and reported what he'd seen to the first policeman he found— the one in Place Macé. Word was sent out. Before long, the women were spotted making for the station at Golfe-Juan. That's a couple of miles from here in the other direction, over toward Cannes."

"Did they still have the suitcases?"

"They'd dropped one on the way. It was found yesterday in a clump of tamarisks. . . . They were upset, and found it hard to explain their conduct. They said they were hurrying to see a sick relative in Lyon. But the man who caught them was smart enough to ask them to open their bags. And what did he find but a pack of bonds, some large-denomination notes, and other valuables!

"It was apéritif time, and a large crowd was gathering. It escorted the two women, first to the police station and then to the local jail, where they were locked up for the night."

"The house was searched?"

"First thing next morning. Nothing was found. The two women pretended they didn't know what had become of Brown. Around noon, a gardener pointed out a place where the earth had recently been dug up. And a couple of inches deep they found Brown's body, fully dressed."

"What did the two women say to that?"

"They changed their tune at once. What they said now was that, three days before, Brown had driven up to the house. They were surprised when he didn't put the car away at once. Gina looked out the window and saw him staggering up the garden path. She thought he was drunk. . . . Then he fell full length on the front steps."

"Dead, of course."

"As dead as could be. When we examined the body, we found he'd been stabbed between the shoulder blades."

"And they kept him in the house with them for three days?"

"Yes. And they can't give any plausible reason for it. They claim that Brown hated everything to do with the police.

"They buried him and took to their heels, with the money and the bonds and all the valuables they could carry. . . . I understand why the car stood there on the road for three days. Gina could hardly drive. She'd had a few lessons, but wasn't up to backing the car into the garage."

The two men moved into the living room.

"Was there any blood in the car?"

"Not a sign. They swear they washed it off."

"Is that all?"

"Yes. Except that they're furious and demand to be released. They've been moved to Antibes now."

The horse outside neighed. Maigret, who had smoked his cigar almost to the end, looked around for a place to get rid of it.

6

"Have some whiskey while you're here," said Boutigues as his eye lighted on a liquor cabinet.

No. Somehow the story fell flat. For the life of him, Maigret could not take it seriously. It was the fault of the sunshine and the oranges and mimosa, and that fisherman, who was still plunging his reed into the clear water, aiming at the sea urchins so far below.

"Can you leave the keys with me?"

"Certainly, now that you're taking over the investigation."

Maigret swallowed his whiskey, looked idly at the record on the phonograph, and fiddled with the knobs of the radio, which at once responded:

". . . wheat at the close . . . November . . ."

At the same moment he caught sight of a photograph next to the radio. He picked it up to study it.

"Is this he?"

"Yes . . . though I never saw him alive myself."

Maigret switched off the radio with a touch of impatience. Something had clicked inside him. Interest? More than that. A confused sensation, and disagreeable besides. Before, Brown had been merely Brown, an unknown stranger who had come to a bad and somewhat mysterious end. The sort of man he had been, what he had thought, felt, and suffered, were questions that had not come up.

And now, suddenly, looking at the photograph, Maigret was troubled by the feeling that the person it showed him was someone he knew. Yet someone he had never set eyes on—of that he felt quite sure.

The broad face gave an impression of health; the complexion must have been ruddy. The hair was getting thin; the mustache was close-clipped; the eyes were large and clear. . . .

But it wasn't the features in themselves that struck him. It

7

was something vaguer, more general. It was the expression. There was something in the expression that resembled Maigret himself. The same look of almost exaggerated calm. The same good-natured irony about the mouth. And the line of the shoulders, slightly hunched . . .

Brown the corpse was forgotten. Here was a man who intrigued Maigret, whether Maigret liked it or not, a man he must know more about.

"Another shot of whiskey, Superintendent? It's not too bad."

Boutigues was in a relaxed mood. But if Maigret had been none too responsive before, he was less so now, looking around with an absent stare. Boutigues did not know what to make of him.

"Shall we give the driver a glass?"

"No. We're leaving."

"You won't look through the house?"

"Another time."

He'd go over the place alone, and when his brain wasn't humming with sunshine. On the way back, he was silent, merely nodding at Boutigues' remarks. Boutigues began to wonder what he'd done to offend him.

"You must see the Old Town. . . . The jail's next to the market . . . Early morning is really the best time for . . ."

"Which hotel?" asked the driver, turning around.

"Perhaps you'd like to be right in the center," Boutigues suggested.

"Leave me here. This'll do."

They were just coming to a modest hotel, more a family pension. It was halfway between Antibes and the Cap.

"Will you be coming to the jail tonight?"

"Tomorrow, more likely, but I'll see."

"Should I pick you up? But perhaps you'd like to go to the casino at Juan-les-Pins. After dinner, I mean. I'd be . . ."

8

"Thanks, but I'm too tired."

He wasn't really tired. He simply wasn't in the mood. He was hot, sweaty. In his room, which faced the sea, he turned on the water for a bath, then changed his mind and went downstairs again, his pipe between his teeth, his hands in his pockets.

As he went out, he had a glimpse of the dining room—little white tables, napkins folded like fans and stuck into the glasses, bottles of wine and mineral water, a waitress sweeping.

Brown had been killed by a knife thrust in the back, and his "two women" had made off with the money. . . .

But this still formed no image in his mind. Instead, his eyes wandered aimlessly to where the sun was slowly sinking, and then along the whole stretch of the horizon to Nice, where the Promenade des Anglais was just visible as a white line. Turning his back on the sea, he stared at the mountaintops still covered with snow.

Facing the sea once more, he silently recited his lesson:

"Nice on the left, about fifteen miles away; Cannes on the right, to the west, less than seven . . ."

It was a little world, a narrow strip between the mountains and the Mediterranean—a world of simmering sunshine, strange flowers, feverish flies, the scent of mimosa, cars gliding on soft asphalt; a world whose center for him was the villa where Brown had lived with his women.

Maigret couldn't face the half-mile walk into town. So he went back into the Hotel Bacon, and from there telephoned the jail.

"Can I speak to the warden?"

"He's on vacation."

"His deputy, then?"

"There isn't one. There's only me."

"All right. Bring the two women prisoners to their villa—say, an hour from now."

The guard's head must have been full of sunshine, too, or perhaps he'd been drinking, because he forgot to ask Maigret for a warrant.

He merely said: "Yes . . . And you'll return them to us . . . ?"

Maigret yawned, stretched, and refilled his pipe. Even the pipe didn't taste the same down here!

Brown had been killed, and the two women . . . It was becoming a refrain.

He strolled toward the villa. When he came to where the car had crashed, he almost laughed. Just the place for a beginner. The struggle with the gears, the car jerking forward, and then the sharp bend coming before she'd had time to recover.

He could see it perfectly. The butcher coming up behind in the twilight. . . . The two women trying to run with three suitcases and finally abandoning the heaviest among some tamarisks by the roadside.

A limousine passed, driven by a chauffeur. In the back an Indian face—no doubt the maharajah. The blue of the sea was darkening, except at the sunset, where it became orange and then red. Lights were switched on, pale in the dusk.

Maigret, alone in the evening vastness, quietly walked up to the garden gate like a man returning home. He unlocked it, left it open, and went to the front door. The trees were full of birds. The creak of the door must have been a familiar sound to Brown.

Inside, Maigret sniffed. Every house has its own peculiar smell. What predominated in this one was a strong perfume, probably musk, though it was somewhat obscured by the cigars he and Boutigues had smoked that afternoon. He went into the living room, switched on the light, and sat down between the radio and the phonograph. The chair must have been Brown's, because it was the one that showed the most signs of wear.

He had been stabbed, and the two women . . .

The light was dim, but Maigret saw there was another lamp, one with a huge pink silk shade. When he switched that on, too, the room came to life.

During the war Brown had worked for the Deuxième Bureau. That's why the local papers had pounced so eagerly on the affair. For the public, espionage was always mysterious and full of glamour. Maigret had looked at some of the absurd headlines during the last part of his journey:

INTERNATIONAL PLOT

A SECOND KOTIOUPOFF AFFAIR

SPY DRAMA

Some papers thought they could detect the hand of the KGB; others that of the CIA or the SIS.

Maigret looked around. Something seemed wrong with the room. Of course: The large bay window, with the blackening night outside. He got up and closed the curtains.

He tried to picture an ordinary evening in this room.

Say, one of the women sewing over there . . .

There was, in fact, some embroidery lying on a little table.

And the other in that corner . . . where a book was lying—
The Passions of Rudolph Valentino.

But that was as far as he could get. He'd have to wait for Gina and her mother. Listening intently, he could just hear the sea hitting the rocks below. He took another look at Brown's photograph, which was signed by a photographer in Nice.

"Tactful handling and no trouble!"

In other words, find out the truth as quickly as possible, to keep it hushed up, and stop the wild rumors of reporters and public.

There were footsteps on the gravel path, and a bell in the hall rang with a low, musical note. Opening the front door, Maigret saw two women with a man in uniform.

"Thank you. You can go. I'll take charge of the ladies. . . . Come in, will you?"

They might have been his guests. He hadn't yet seen their features, but his nose immediately caught a strong whiff of musk.

"I hope that at last they've realized . . ." began the mother, in a croaky, broken voice.

"Of course, of course. Do make yourselves at home."

They entered the lighted room. The mother's face, wrinkled, was covered with a thick coat of make-up. Standing in the middle of the room, she looked around, as though to assure herself that nothing was missing.

The other woman, more on the defensive, looked warily at Maigret while arranging the folds of her dress and assuming a smile that was meant to be winning.

"Is it true they've brought you all the way from Paris?"

"Do take off your coats . . . Sit down as you would any other evening."

They couldn't quite understand. They were at home; yet at the same time they weren't. They were afraid of walking into a trap.

"We're going to have a little talk, the three of us."

"Have you learned anything?"

It was the daughter who asked the question, and her mother quickly snapped at her:

"Take care, Gina!"

Even now that the work was beginning, Maigret found it hard to take his part seriously. The old woman was horrible to look at, in spite of her makeup—or perhaps because of it.

As for Gina, her ample figure was almost too buxom. In her dark silk dress, she obviously meant to be a femme fatale, but it didn't quite come off.

And that perfume . . . What he had smelled before was nothing. The air in the room now reeked with musk. It was like the smell in certain little theaters.

There was no drama, no mystery. Just a mother who did embroidery while keeping an eye on her daughter. And a daughter who read about the loves of Rudolph Valentino.

Maigret, who had resumed his place in Brown's chair, looked at them without expression and asked himself, with a shade of embarrassment:

How the devil could Brown put up with these two women?

Ten years! Long days of ceaseless sunshine laden with the scent of mimosa, and that unbroken stretch of blue sea. And ten years of long evenings, with the radio his only deliverance from the silence of the mother and her needlework and the daughter reading under the pink lampshade.

Unconsciously, Maigret's hand felt for the photograph of the dead man who'd had the nerve to look like him!

CHAPTER TWO

A Talk about Brown

"What did he do with himself in the evening?"

Maigret, with his legs crossed, was bored. He was bored mainly with the old woman, who kept playing the great lady.

"We seldom went out. . . . As a rule, my daughter read, while I . . ."

"Let's talk about Brown!"

At that she was offended, and answered curtly:

"He did nothing."

"He listened to the radio," sighed Gina, lolling in her chair with assumed nonchalance. "The fonder one is of real music, the more one hates . . ."

"Let's talk about Brown! Was his health good?"

"If he had taken my advice," began the mother, "he'd never have been bothered by his liver or his kidneys. . . . When a man's past forty . . ."

Maigret looked like a host listening politely to the prize

bore, who laughs so much at his own story he can't finish it. They were both ridiculous—the mother with her pretentious airs; the daughter posing like an odalisque.

"You told the police he returned in his car, that evening, walked up the garden path, and then fell on the front steps."

"Yes. Like a man dead drunk," answered Gina. "I shouted to him from the window that he could come into the house when he was sober again."

"Did he often come home drunk?"

The mother answered:

"If you only knew how patient we've been during the last ten years . . ."

"Did he often come home drunk?"

"Whenever he went off—or nearly every time . . . We called them his bouts."

"And these bouts were frequent?"

Maigret couldn't help smiling. He felt relieved. So Brown hadn't, after all, spent every evening of those ten years sitting with these two women!

"Generally once a month."

"How long did they last?"

"He'd be away three days, four days, or sometimes longer. . . . And when he came back, he'd be dirty and stinking of alcohol."

"But you let him go off again the next month?"

Silence. The mother stiffened and gave the superintendent a sharp look.

"But surely the two of you had some influence over him?"

"We couldn't stop him from going to get the money."

"And you couldn't go with him?"

Gina stood up.

"This is all very painful," she said with a sigh and a look of weariness. "But I must explain the situation, Superinten-

16

dent. . . . You see, we weren't married. . . . Of course, William always treated me as his wife, even to the point of having *Maman* live with us. . . . And I was known to the people here as Madame Brown. . . . Otherwise, I would never have accepted . . ."

"Neither would I," added the other.

"Still, it was never quite the same thing. I don't want to speak ill of William . . . but on one point, one point only, there was a difference: the question of money."

"Was he rich?"

"I don't know."

"And you don't know where the money came from, either? . . . That's why you let him go off every month: to get his money?"

"I tried to follow him—I admit. . . . But didn't I have a right to? . . . He was on his guard, though, and he always took the car."

Maigret was relaxed now, and was beginning to be amused. He was reconciled to this joker Brown, who could live for ten years with these two harpies without letting them find out the size or the source of his income.

"Did he bring back a lot each time?"

"Hardly enough to keep us going a month. During the last week, we'd have a hard time making ends meet."

It was a sore spot. Merely thinking about it made them both furious.

When funds got low, they would begin to watch William anxiously, for signs of an incipient bout. But they couldn't very well say to him:

"Run along now and have your little binge."

No doubt they dropped hints. Maigret could easily imagine that.

"Who did he give the money to?"

17

"To *Maman*," said Gina.

"She did the housekeeping."

"Of course. And the cooking, too. There wasn't enough money to keep a servant."

Then, the trick was played. Toward the end of the month, the most impossible meals would be served, and if Brown said anything, they had only to answer:

"It's all we can manage on the money that's left."

Would it take a lot to get him moving? Or was he only too glad of the excuse to get away?

"What time of day would he leave?"

"Any time. He'd be out in the garden or in the garage working on the car, and suddenly we'd hear him start the motor. . . ."

"And you tried to follow him . . . in a taxi?"

"Yes, once. But William lost us in the little streets of Antibes. . . . I know where he kept the car. In a garage in Cannes . . . It stayed there all the time he was away."

"So he might have gone from there by train to Paris, or anywhere else?"

"Perhaps."

"Or he might have stayed in the area?"

"We've never heard of anybody seeing him."

"And it was when he returned from a bout that he was killed?"

"Yes . . . He was away a whole week."

"Did you find the money on him?"

"The same amount as usual—two thousand francs."

"If you ask me," the old woman said, "I think his monthly income was much larger than that. Four thousand, perhaps, or even five . . . He preferred, apparently, to squander the rest of it by himself, leaving little for us."

Maigret leaned back sanctimoniously in Brown's easy chair. As questions and answers followed each other, his smile grew broader.

"Was he selfish?"

"William? He was the best of men."

"Tell me about your everyday habits. Who got up first?"

"William. More often than not he slept downstairs on a couch, and we'd hear him moving around early. Sometimes it was hardly light. . . . Over and over I said to him . . ."

"Excuse me! Did he make the coffee?"

"Yes. Though it was always cold when we came down at ten."

"What would he be doing then?"

"Puttering . . . In the garden . . . or in the garage . . . Sometimes he went and sat on the beach. And then there was the shopping. He'd take us in the car. And that's another thing: I could never get him to dress properly first. He would go in his slippers and without even brushing his hair. Anybody could see his nightshirt underneath his jacket. And he'd be like that right in the middle of Antibes, waiting for us outside the shops."

"He dressed before lunch?"

"Sometimes, sometimes not! He's gone as long as five days without washing."

"Where did you eat?"

"In the kitchen. When you have no help in the house, you can't have crumbs in all the rooms."

"And in the afternoon?"

In the afternoon, the two women napped. Then, near five o'clock, his slippers could be heard. . . .

"Quarrels?"

"Hardly ever. Though I must say William had an aggra-

19

vating habit of simply ignoring you when you spoke to him."

Maigret refrained from laughing. But he was beginning to feel quite friendly toward this damn Brown.

"Then somebody killed him. . . . Could it have been before he entered the garden? . . . But then you would have found blood in the car."

"We have no reason not to tell the truth."

"Of course not. So, he was killed elsewhere. Or, rather, wounded. And instead of going to a doctor or the police, he ended up here. . . . You carried the body inside?"

"We couldn't very well leave it outside!"

"Now, tell me why you didn't inform the authorities. I'm sure you have an excellent reason."

"Yes, monsieur," answered the old woman, jumping up from her chair, "and I'd like you to know it. In any case, you'll find out all about Brown sooner or later. . . . You see, he was already married, long ago in Australia. . . . He was Australian. His wife's still living. For reasons best known to her, she would never divorce him. It's her fault we do not live in the finest villa on the Côte d'Azur."

"You've seen her?"

"She's never left Australia. . . . But she managed all right from where she was. She had her husband declared incompetent. . . . These ten years, we've been looking after him, trying to make up for all he's suffered. . . . And thanks to us, there's a little money put aside. . . . But if . . ."

"If Madame Brown heard of her husband's death, she could seize everything, since she's still legally his wife."

"Exactly. We would have sacrificed ourselves for nothing! And not only that! I'm not by any means penniless myself. My husband was in the army, and I get a small pension. A lot of the things in the house are my property, but it wouldn't be easy to prove it. She'd have the law on her side if she wanted to take the house and everything in it and put us out on the street."

"So you hesitated. For three days you turned it over in your minds, while the body lay there on the couch. . . . "

"Only two days. Then we buried it."

"But you thought things over for another twenty-four hours, and finally gathered up whatever valuables you could and . . . Incidentally, where were you going?"

"Anywhere. Brussels, London . . ."

"Had you ever driven the car before?" Maigret asked Gina.

"Never! But I once started it in the garage."

Real heroism. What a scene—the departure, the body in the garden, the three heavy suitcases, and the lurching car. . . .

Maigret had had about enough: the atmosphere of the house, the smell of musk, and the rose-colored light shed by the pink lampshade.

"You don't mind my having a look through the house?"

They had recovered their self-possession and dignity, though they were puzzled and perhaps a little disconcerted by this superintendent who took it all so calmly, who seemed, in fact, to regard the whole business as natural.

"You'll excuse the disorder?"

Indeed, it was untidy, though that was hardly the right word. Sordid would be better. There was something of the pigsty about it, mixed with bourgeois pretention.

An old coat of Brown's hung on the stand in the hall. Maigret, going through the pockets, discovered a worn pair of gloves, a key, and a box of cachous.

"He ate cachous?"

"When he'd been drinking—so that we wouldn't smell it on his breath. . . . We were always telling him not to drink whiskey. We often hid the bottle."

21

Above the stand was a stag's head with large antlers. To one side of it was a bamboo table with a silver salver for visiting cards.

"Was he wearing that coat?"

"No. His raincoat."

The dining-room shutters were closed. The room was evidently used only for storage. Brown had apparently been a fisherman, judging by the lobster pots on the floor.

Then the kitchen, where the main stove was never lit. All the cooking had been done on an alcohol burner. On the floor beside it were several dozen empty mineral-water bottles.

"You see, the water here is so full of chalk . . ."

The stair carpet was worn, the brass stair rods tarnished. Gina's room could be found with eyes shut, merely by following the trail of musk! Dresses had been thrown on the unmade bed. Gina had hurriedly gone through them to pick out the best.

There was no bathroom; not even a dressing room.

Maigret preferred not to go into the mother's room.

"We left in such a rush. . . . I'm ashamed to show you the house in such a state."

"I'll come see you again."

"Does that mean we're free?"

"Well, you won't go back to the jail . . . at least for the moment. . . . But if you try to leave Antibes . . ."

"We wouldn't dream of it!"

They accompanied him to the front door.

"A cigar, Superintendent?" said the old woman in her most ladylike voice.

But Gina went further. She couldn't go wrong in trying to win the sympathy of so influential a man.

"Take the whole box. William will never smoke them."

They were too good to be true, the pair of them! When he

got outside, Maigret almost felt drunk. He did not know whether to laugh or grind his teeth.

From the garden gate, the villa presented another aspect altogether—so restfully white against the trees and bushes. The moon had reached one corner of the roof. To the right were the glittering sea and the quivering mimosas.

With his raincoat over his arm, he walked back to the Hotel Bacon, pensive but not really thinking. A host of vague impressions drifted through his mind, some of them disagreeable, others comic.

What a character, that William!

It was getting late. There was nobody in the dining room except one of the maids, who was reading a newspaper. And suddenly Maigret noticed that it wasn't his raincoat over his arm, but Brown's, a filthy thing covered with grease spots.

In the left pocket was a wrench, in the other a handful of small change and some square brass counters marked with a number, the kind used in slot machines found in common little bars.

Maigret counted them. There were ten.

"Hello. This is Inspector Boutigues. Would you like me to pick you up at your hotel?"

It was nine in the morning. From six o'clock on, Maigret had been dozing luxuriously, conscious of the Mediterranean spread out before his window.

"What for?"

"Don't you want to see the body?"

"Yes . . . No . . . This afternoon perhaps. Call me at lunchtime, all right?"

The first thing to do was to wake up. He was in that delicious state of morning sleepiness in which the events of the day

23

before seem hardly real. The two women, for instance. Vague as a dream, or, rather, a nightmare.

They wouldn't be getting up yet. And if Brown were alive, he'd be puttering around in the garage or the garden. All by himself. Unshaved and unwashed. And the coffee, getting colder and colder in the kitchen.

As he dressed, Maigret caught sight of the brass counters. They were in a little heap on the mantelpiece. He had to make an effort to remember where they fit in.

Brown had gone on one of his periodic bouts and was stabbed just before driving home, during the drive, or while walking up to the house, or inside it.

When his right cheek was shaved clean, Maigret started muttering.

"Brown certainly didn't frequent the little bars in Antibes. If he had, Boutigues would have told me."

And hadn't Gina discovered that he kept the car in Cannes?

A quarter of an hour later, he was telephoning the Cannes police.

"Superintendent Maigret, of the Police Judiciaire . . . Can you give me a list of all the bars that have those slot machines?"

"They've all been done away with. An order came out a couple of months ago, and they're illegal now. You won't find one left on the Côte d'Azur."

Maigret went downstairs and asked where he could get a taxi.

"Where do you want to go?"

"Cannes."

"You don't need a taxi for that. There's a bus from Place Macé every three minutes."

So there was. In the morning sunshine, Place Macé was even livelier than the day before. Maigret thought of Brown there, having brought his two women shopping, with his night-shirt showing above his jacket.

He took the bus, and half an hour later was in Cannes looking for the garage Gina had mentioned. He found it near the Boulevard de la Croisette. Everything here seemed white: hotels, shops, trousers and dresses, sails on the sea. It might have been a theater set, a charming fairyland in blue and white.

"Is this where Monsieur Brown used to leave his car?"

"That's right."

"What can you tell me?"

"There! I said it would mean trouble for us as soon as I read he'd been killed. . . . But I don't know anything. I've nothing to hide. . . . He'd simply bring it here one day and come get it again four or five days later."

"Drunk?"

"That's how I knew him best."

"And you don't know where he went?"

"When? While the car was here? Not the slightest."

"And you cleaned it up and kept it in running order?"

"Not at all. In fact, it's been a whole year since the oil was changed."

"What did you think of him?"

The man shrugged his shoulders.

"Nothing at all."

"Eccentric?"

"There are so many eccentric people on the Riviera one gets used to them. Yesterday, for instance, an American girl came in here. Wanted a new body for her car—in the shape of a swan! Well, it's her business, isn't it? She pays the bill."

Maigret had drawn a blank. He had only the brass counters

to help him now. By the harbor he went into a bar frequented by sailors belonging to the yachts.

"Have you got a slot machine?"

"They're prohibited. Two months ago . . . But they're bringing out a new version. It'll be two or three months before they're stopped, too."

"There are none left anywhere?"

The answer was neither yes nor no, but:

"What can I get you?"

Maigret asked for a vermouth. He looked at the line of yachts moored in the harbor, and then at the sailors in the bar and the yachts' names in red letters on their shirts.

"Did you know Brown?"

"What Brown? The one who was killed? . . . He never came here."

"Where did he go?"

With a vague negative gesture, the landlord moved over to serve some other customers. Although it was only March, everybody was perspiring—the smell of summer.

"I once heard someone talking about him," the landlord said, a bottle in his hand, "but I can't remember who it was."

"Never mind. What I'm after is a slot machine."

Brown's women no doubt went through his pockets when he returned from a bout, so the brass counters probably dated from the last one. They'd had other things to think of then.

But it was all so nebulous. And then, this blazing sunshine made Maigret want to sit peacefully on a café terrace, like other people, and watch the boats hardly moving on the calm sea.

Creamy-yellow streetcars . . . Fancy cars . . . He found

himself on the main shopping street of the town, parallel to the Croisette. But what was the use of that?

"If Brown had his bouts in Cannes," he mumbled, "it certainly wasn't here."

He walked on and on, stopping now and again at a bar, where he'd have a vermouth and a chat about slot machines.

"It's not the first time they've been stopped—nor the last either! It only means we have to have a new kind every three or four months. . . ."

"Know anything about Brown?"

"The Brown who was killed?"

It was monotonous. Twelve o'clock struck, and the sun's rays beat mercilessly down on the streets. Maigret felt like going up to a policeman, like a tourist, and asking:

"Where does one go to have some fun?"

If Madame Maigret could see him, she would think that his eyes shone a bit too brightly. All those vermouths.

He turned one corner, then another. And suddenly it was no longer Cannes—at least not the Cannes of the white hotels. This was quite a different world, a world of narrow alleys with lines for laundry stretching overhead from one side to the other.

Two bars, facing each other. On the right, TRUE SAILORS. On the left, LIBERTY BAR.

Maigret went into the one on the right and, standing at the zinc counter, ordered a vermouth.

"That's funny! I thought you had a slot machine."

"We *had*!"

Maigret's head was heavy and his legs felt weak.

"Some places have them still."

"Yes. *Some* have," said the barman acidly as he wiped the

counter. "There's always some that take no notice. Only, that's none of our business, is it?"

He shot a glance opposite. Maigret threw some money on the counter.

"How much?"

"That's it. Two francs twenty-five."

Maigret walked across to the Liberty Bar and pushed open the door.

CHAPTER THREE

William's Goddaughter

There was nobody in the bar, which was very small—hardly
more than six feet by ten. It was two steps below street level.
A narrow counter. A shelf with a dozen glasses on it. The
slot machine. Two tables.

In the back was a glass-paneled door by a covered curtain.
Through it Maigret could make out some heads turned toward
him. But nobody got up to greet the customer. There was only
a woman's voice calling out:

"What are you standing there for?"

Maigret entered the room behind, going down another step.
The room was so low that the bottom of the window was flush
with the stones of the back yard. In the dim light he saw three
people sitting at a table.

The woman who had called out went on eating, with her
elbows on the table. But at the same time she looked at Mai-

gret, exactly the way he looked at people, placidly but taking in every detail.

At last, with a jerk of her chin, she directed him to a stool and sighed.

"You've taken long enough."

On one side of her was a man in nautical uniform. Maigret could see only his back and his fair hair, clipped short at the neck.

"Eat," the woman said to him. "There's nothing to worry about."

On her other side, facing Maigret, sat a girl with a pale complexion and large mistrustful eyes.

She was hardly covered by her dressing gown. The whole of one breast was visible, but nobody seemed to notice.

"Sit down. You don't mind if we go on with our lunch?"

Was she forty-five, fifty? Perhaps more, but it was difficult to say. Fat, smiling, self-confident, she was obviously afraid of no one; she had seen all there was to see and felt all there was to feel.

One glance had told her what Maigret had come for. And she hadn't even moved from her seat. She cut half a dozen thick slices from a leg of mutton. Maigret had rarely seen mutton so juicy and tender.

"I suppose you come from Nice? Or Antibes? I've never seen you before."

"From Paris. Superintendent, Police Judiciaire."

"Ah!"

And this "Ah" made it clear she understood the difference and appreciated her visitor's rank.

"So it's true, then?"

"What?"

30

"That William was some kind of important person."

Maigret could see the man's profile now. He wasn't an ordinary sailor. His uniform was of fine material, and had gold braid. On his hat was the insigne of a yacht club. He seemed embarrassed at being found there and kept his eyes studiously on his plate.

"Who is he?"

"We all call him Yan. I don't know his real name. He's the steward on the *Ardena*, a Swedish yacht that comes here every winter. That's right, Yan, isn't it? Steward? Monsieur is from the police. . . . I told you about William."

The other nodded, though he hardly seemed to understand.

"He says yes, but he has only a vague idea of what's said to him. Not much French . . . He's a nice fellow, and has a wife and kids at home. . . . Show the photo, Yan. Photo . . . yes."

Yan produced a photograph from his jacket. It showed a young woman sitting outside a door with two babies on the lawn at her feet.

"Twins," explained the hostess. "Yan comes and has a meal with us from time to time. He likes it here: gives him a sort of family feeling. He brought the mutton and the peaches."

Maigret turned toward the girl, who hadn't bothered to close her dressing gown.

"And this . . . ?"

"This is Sylvie, William's goddaughter."

"Goddaughter?"

"Oh, not in church. He wasn't at her baptism. . . . In fact, were you baptized, Sylvie?"

"Certainly," answered Sylvie, still looking at Maigret with suspicion while she toyed with her food.

"William was fond of her. She'd tell him all her troubles, and he'd comfort her."

Maigret was sitting on the stool, his elbows on his knees and his chin in his hands. The fat woman prepared the salad, first rubbing the bowl with garlic. It looked like a masterpiece.

"Have you had your lunch?"

He lied.

"Yes . . . I . . ."

"If not, just say so. We don't stand on ceremony here. . . . That's right, Yan, isn't it? . . . Look at him! He says yes even though he doesn't understand. . . . I love them all, these boys from the North."

She tasted the salad thoughtfully and added another dash of an olive oil that smelled delicious. There was no tablecloth, and the table was none too clean. Stairs led from the kitchen itself to a floor above. A sewing machine stood in one corner.

The yard outside was bathed in sunshine, so much so that the little window made a blinding rectangle of light. In contrast, they seemed to be in a cool twilight.

"You can ask your questions. Sylvie knows as much as I do. As for Yan . . ."

"How long have you had this bar?"

"Maybe fifteen years . . . I was married to an Englishman, who was an acrobat, so all the English sailors used to come here. Music-hall people, too . . . He died nine years ago, drowned in a regatta. He was racing for a titled lady who had three yachts. I'll remember her name in a minute. You'll know it."

"What happened then?"

"Nothing. I simply kept the place."

"Do you have many customers?"

"I don't want many. . . . They're more friends than customers. Like Yan, like William. They know I'm alone and that I like company. So they drop in to split a bottle with me.

. . . Sometimes they bring a chicken or a fish or two, and we have a meal together."

As she was refilling the glasses, she realized that Maigret had none.

"Get a glass for the superintendent, Sylvie."

The girl, her bare feet in slippers and her body obviously covered only by the dressing gown, got up without a word and went into the bar, brushing past Maigret on her way without a word of excuse. The older woman took advantage of her absence to say:

"Don't take any notice. She adored Will . . . So it's been a dreadful blow."

"She sleeps here?"

"Sometimes, sometimes not."

"What does she do?"

The woman looked reproachfully at Maigret, as if to say:

"You, a member of the Police Judiciaire, can ask that question?"

The next moment she was saying:

"Oh, she's a good girl. No harm in her at all."

"Did William know?"

The same reproachful look. Had she made a mistake about Maigret? Couldn't he understand? Or must she dot the *i*'s?

Yan had finished eating. He seemed to be preparing to say something, but it wasn't necessary.

"Yes, Yan, you can go now. . . . Will you come this evening?"

"If my people go to the Casino."

He stood up, but hesitated to go through the customary ritual. The woman, however, lifted her face, and he bent down and planted a kiss on her forehead, blushing at the same time because of Maigret's presence. As he turned, he met Sylvie returning with a glass.

33

"Going?"

"Yes."

And he kissed her on the forehead, too, nodded awkwardly to Maigret, tripped over the step, and literally dived into the bar and out into the street, straightening his cap as he hurried away.

"He's a nice boy. Docsn't like carrying on with the other yacht crews. Just likes to sit here quietly . . ."

She had finished eating and was leaning forward on her elbows.

"Will you pour the coffee, Sylvie?"

Hardly a sound came from the street. It might have been any time of the day or night if it hadn't been for that rectangle of sunshine and the alarm clock in the middle of the mantelpiece ticking out the hours.

"Well now, what exactly do you want to know? . . . Here's good health to you anyhow! . . . This is William's whiskey."

"What's your name?"

"Jaja. Sometimes, to tease me, they call me Fat Jaja."

She looked down at her enormous bosom resting on the table.

"Did you know William for long?"

"Seems like I've known him always. But I never knew his last name till a few days ago. . . . I ought to tell you that the Liberty Bar was quite famous in my husband's day. Because of the music-hall people. They attracted a rich clientele, who came to rub shoulders with them.

"The yachting crowd came more than anybody. They like out-of-the-way places like this. And they're always ready for fun. . . . I remember William in those days. Saw him several times. All dressed up in a white cap and with a pretty girl on each arm . . .

"Yes, that crowd drank champagne into the small hours,

34

and offered drinks to anyone who happened to be here. . . .

"And then he died—I mean my husband. I shut the place for a month. . . . Anyhow, it wasn't the season. . . . And then, the next winter, I spent three weeks in the hospital with peritonitis.

"When I came out, I found someone had grabbed the chance and opened a place right opposite. . . .

"Since then it's been quiet here. But then, I don't care about having a lot of customers."

Sylvie, her chin resting on her hand, never took her eyes off Maigret. The sleeve of her dressing gown was hanging in her plate.

"One day I saw William again, and it was from that time that I really got to know him. . . . We drank, told stories half the night. In the end, I put him to bed on the couch, because he could never have gotten home."

"He still had his yachtsman's cap?"

"No. He was not the same man. Liquor no longer made him laugh. . . . And since then, he dropped in on me from time to time."

"Did you know his address?"

"No. And I'm not one to ask questions. He never talked about his affairs at all."

"How long did he stay?"

"Three or four days, mostly. . . . He'd bring food with him—or sometimes he'd give me some money to go shopping . . . He used to swear he never had such good meals as here."

Looking at the pink meat of the mutton and the remains of the fragrant salad, Maigret could easily believe it.

"Was Sylvie with you then?"

"What are you thinking? She's only twenty-one now."

"How did you come to know her?"

A sullen look came into Sylvie's face, but Jaja said to her:

"Come now! The superintendent knows what's what. . . . It was one evening when William was here. Just him and me alone. And then Sylvie came in with a couple of men, salesmen or something of the sort. They were already half soused when they arrived, and they started tossing it down harder than ever. . . . As for her, you could tell at a glance she was new. She wanted to get them away before they were really drunk, but she didn't know how to do it. . . . Of course you can guess what happened. They forgot all about her. Finally they went off, leaving her behind. . . . She cried. She told us she'd come from Paris for the season and hadn't even enough money to pay for a bed. So I let her sleep with me. . . . Now she stays when she wants to; it became a habit."

"A habit!" growled Maigret.

Jaja beamed.

"What do you expect? I keep open house. And here we don't worry. We take each day as it comes."

She was quite sincere. Her eyes fell on the girl's breast, and she sighed:

"Pity her health isn't better. You can see her ribs sticking out. William wanted to pay for her to go into a sanatorium, but she wouldn't hear of it."

"Were she and William . . . ?"

It was Sylvie herself who answered, angrily:

"Never. It's not true."

And Fat Jaja explained as she sipped her coffee:

"He wasn't a man for that. Particularly with her . . . I won't say that, now and then . . ."

"Women?"

"He'd pick women up . . . But it was rare. It didn't interest him."

"When did he leave you last Friday?"

"Right after lunch. We finished about two, like today."

"Did he say where he was going?"

"He never did."

"Was Sylvie here?"

"She left five minutes before."

"To go where?" asked Maigret, turning to the girl.

"What a question!" she snarled contemptuously.

"Down to the harbor? Is that where you . . . ?"

"There, anywhere."

"Was anyone else here?"

"Nobody . . . It was hot that afternoon. I fell asleep in my chair and napped for a whole hour."

It had been after five when William arrived at the villa in Antibes with his car.

"Did he go to other bars like this?"

"None! Besides, there are no other bars like this."

Obviously. Maigret himself, who had been there only an hour, felt this. It was difficult to say what gave him the feeling. The casual, impersonal hospitality? The atmosphere of indolence and relaxation?

It was the kind of place where you had to make an effort of will to get up and leave. Time passed slowly. The hands of the clock crept around its drab white face. The rectangle of sun shifted.

"I read about it in the papers. The name Brown meant nothing to me, but I recognized his photograph. . . . We cried, Sylvie and me. . . . What could he want with those two women? . . . But of course in our situation it's best to stay away from trouble. . . . But I thought the police would turn up sooner or later. When I saw you coming out of the True Sailors, I had no doubt."

She spoke slowly, filling the glasses. She sipped at hers.

"Whoever did it is a skunk, because there aren't many men in the world like William. . . . I know!"

"He never talked to you about his past?"

She sighed. Didn't he understand that this was just the place where one *didn't* talk about the past?

"All I can tell you is that he was a gentleman, a man who had been very rich, and still was, maybe. . . . I don't know. . . . He'd had a yacht and lots of people to wait on him."

"Was he sad?"

Again she sighed.

"Can't you understand? . . . You've seen Yan. Would you call him sad? . . . But Yan's different. . . . Would you say I am sad? Perhaps you would. . . . What one likes is to drink, talk a lot of nonsense, and then have a good cry. . . ."

Sylvie looked at her disapprovingly. But then, she was drinking coffee, whereas Fat Jaja was already on her third glass of whiskey.

"I'm glad you came. We've had it all out now. We've got nothing to hide, nothing to reproach ourselves with. . . . But one never knows with the police. . . . Now, if it had been the Cannes police, they'd have taken away my license, I'm sure."

"Did William spend a lot of money?"

Was it hopeless to try to make him understand?

"He did and he didn't. . . . He gave what was needed for food and drink, and now and then he'd pay the gas or the electricity. Or he would give Sylvie a hundred francs to buy stockings with."

Maigret was hungry, and that delicious leg of mutton was only a foot from his nostrils. Two slices still lay on the plate. He picked one up in his fingers and ate it as he went on talking, just as if he was one of the household.

"Does Sylvie bring her customers here?"

"Never! It would give them a good excuse to shut the place up. . . . There are hotels enough for that in Cannes!"

And, looking into Maigret's eyes, she added:

38

"You think it's those two women who . . ."

But she broke off and turned her head. Sylvie also peered through the curtain on the glass-paneled door. The street door had been opened. Someone crossed the bar and came to the kitchen, stopping suddenly in the doorway at the sight of a stranger.

Sylvie stood up. Jaja, rather pink perhaps, said to the new-comer:

"Come in! This is the superintendent who's checking on William."

And then, to Maigret:

"A friend of ours—Joseph. He's a waiter at the Casino."

That could be seen from his gray suit, white collar and shirt front, his black tie and black patent-leather shoes.

"I'll come back later," he said.

"No, no. Come in."

Joseph couldn't make up his mind.

"I just dropped in to say hello, since I was passing. I've got a good tip for the . . ."

"So you play the horses?" asked Maigret, turning slightly toward him.

"Now and then. Sometimes a customer gives me a tip. . . . But I must be running."

And he beat a hasty retreat, though not without making a sign to Sylvie—or so Maigret thought. The girl sat down again.

"He'll lose again," said Jaja, sighing. "He's not a bad fellow, though."

"I must get dressed," said Sylvie, standing up again, and disclosing most of her body. It wasn't meant to be seductive. It simply didn't matter.

She went upstairs, and they could hear her moving around overhead. It seemed to Maigret that Jaja had pricked up her ears.

"She plays the horses, too, sometimes. . . . It's she who's lost most by William's death."

A moment later, Maigret jumped from his seat, quickly crossed the bar, and opened the door to the street. But he wasn't quick enough. Joseph was striding off as fast as he could, without looking behind. From above came the sound of a window being shut.

"What's the matter?" asked Jaja when he returned.

"Nothing. Just an idea."

"Another glass? And if you like the mutton, help yourself."

Sylvie came down, transformed, indeed almost unrecognizable, in a navy-blue tailored skirt, a matching jacket in her hand. She looked fresh and girlish. Under her white silk blouse, her little breasts were enticing. Yet Maigret had regarded them earlier without the least interest. Her skirt was tight, and her tautly stretched stockings showed her legs off well.

"See you this evening."

And she, too, kissed Jaja's forehead. Turning toward Maigret, she hesitated. As if undecided whether to ignore him or spit in his face. But there was no doubt about her attitude. She was hostile.

"I suppose," she said at last, frigidly, "you won't be wanting me any more." She stood stiffly for a moment and then stalked out.

Jaja laughed as once again she filled the glasses.

"Don't pay any attention to her. These young things haven't much sense. . . . Shall I give you a plate, so you can try my salad?"

The empty bar below street level, the half-lit kitchen lower still; upstairs, a bedroom, probably in disorder; and the little window on the back yard, from which the sun had almost disappeared . . .

It was a strange world, and in the middle of it sat Maigret, finishing up the remains of a perfect salad. Facing him was Fat Jaja, who seemed to be supported by her immense bosom, which spread over the table. She sighed.

"When I was her age, I had to mind my *p*'s and *q*'s."

She didn't need to say more. He could very well imagine her in a loud silk dress going up and down somewhere in Paris, near Porte Saint-Denis or in Montmartre, while from the window of some bar her exacting "protector" would keep a watchful eye on her.

"But nowadays . . ."

She had done too much honor to William's whiskey. It was with wet eyes that she looked at Maigret, and her almost childish mouth puckered. Was she going to have a good cry?

"You remind me of William. That's where he always sat. . . . And he used to put his pipe down beside his plate when he ate—just like you. . . . He had the same shoulders. . . . Do you know you look like him?"

She only wiped her eyes. There would be no tears after all.

CHAPTER FOUR

Gentian

The day was drawing to a close. That subtle hour had come when the quality of light is indescribable, when the warm breath of the setting sun is turned cool and lucid by the approaching night. Maigret slipped out of the Liberty Bar much as one might leave a house of ill repute, his hands deep in his pockets, his hat pulled down over his eyes. And then, after a dozen steps, he couldn't help turning around, as though to make sure the place really existed.

Yes, there it was! A narrow front squeezed between two houses, and painted an ugly brown with yellow lettering. Behind the window of the bar a plant was flowering, and beside it on the windowsill was a sleeping cat.

Jaja, too, was no doubt dozing, in the kitchen behind, all alone with the clock counting out the minutes.

At the end of the alley, he found himself back once more

in the everyday world: shops, people dressed alike, cars, a streetcar, and a policeman.

There, on the right, the Croisette, looking exactly like those watercolors the Tourist Bureau used to illustrate pamphlets boosting Cannes.

It was all so gentle and peaceful. People strolled with no fuss, no hurry. Cars glided as though propelled by something subtler than machinery. . . . And all those white yachts floating in the harbor . . .

Maigret felt tired, worn out, yet he had no desire to go back to his hotel. He walked aimlessly, stopping without knowing why, and then walked again. It was as if his will had remained behind in Jaja's cave. Only his body was here; the rest was at that table still littered with the remains of the midday meal, at that table where a correct Swedish steward had sat facing Sylvie's naked breast.

For almost ten years, William Brown had lived three or four days a month in that warm laziness, keeping Jaja company—Jaja, who after a glass or two would talk, and after a few more glasses would have her cry and fall asleep in her chair.

Gentian, of course!

Maigret was delighted. He'd found it: what he'd been looking for the last quarter of an hour without knowing it. Ever since he'd left the Liberty Bar he had been trying to define the place, trying to strip it of its picturesque surface until only its essence remained. Gentian. He remembered what an old friend had said to him once when he'd offered him a drink.

"What would you like?"

"A gentian."

"What's that? A new fashion?"

"No. Hardly a fashion! It's the drunkard's last resource. You never tried it? It's bitter. It's not even strong alcohol. But when you've soaked yourself for thirty years in every drink imaginable, that's all that's left to you. That queer bitter taste is the one thing you can still get a kick out of."

The Liberty Bar was like that. A place without vice, or at least without malice, where nothing had to be explained. A bar where you went straight through to the kitchen and sat down like one of Jaja's family.

And after a drink or two you'd go to the butcher's and bring back a piece of meat, and then you'd drink some more while Jaja put it on to cook. Sylvie would come down with sleepy eyes, half-naked, and you'd kiss her on the forehead without so much as a glance at her little breasts.

The room was dingy and none too clean. You wouldn't talk a lot. The conversation would go on idly, without conviction, like the lives that were spent there.

The busy world was shut out. Only that little rectangle of sunlight . . .

To eat, drink, doze . . . And then start drinking again while Sylvie went upstairs to dress, to pull her stockings tight over her thighs before going off to work. . . .

"See you," she'd say to her "godfather" as she went out.

What would William Brown find in that? What Maigret's pal had found in gentian? Was the Liberty Bar his last resource, the last refuge of a man who had sampled everything, seen everything, and tried every vice?

Women without beauty, who did not even try to look beautiful; women without desire and who were not desired; women you'd kiss gravely on the forehead and give a hundred francs to, for stockings . . . And when they came home, you'd ask:

"How did you do?"

Maigret was depressed. He wanted to think of something else. He stopped and faced the harbor. A thin sheet of mist was spreading, only inches above the water.

45

He had already passed the racing boats and was now opposite the big yachts. A few paces from him a sailor on a white yacht, obviously owned by some pasha, was hauling down a red flag with a white crescent.

Next to that yacht was one not much under a hundred and fifty feet long. On the stern in gilt letters ran the name: *Ardena*.

He thought at once of the Swedish steward at Jaja's and, almost at the same moment, raising his head, he caught sight of him on deck. The steward's white-gloved hands were carrying a tray, which he put down on a wicker table.

The owner was leaning over the side with two girls. When he laughed, he disclosed a splendid set of teeth. There was only a short gangway between them, and Maigret walked up it and went on board. Inwardly he chuckled at the expression on the steward's face.

There are moments like that, when you do something just for the sake of something to do; not because it's useful, but to take your mind off other things.

"Pardon me, monsieur."

The owner stopped laughing. He and the girls turned toward Maigret and waited for him to continue.

"Might I ask whether you know a certain William Brown?"

"He has a boat?"

"He had one. . . . William Brown . . ."

Maigret hardly bothered to listen for the answer. He gazed at the man in front of him, a truly aristocratic-looking Swede, who appeared to be about forty-five. And seeing him there with those two women, he thought:

Brown was like that! He, too, had been surrounded with beautiful girls, whose pretty dresses showed just enough of their figures to excite desire. To amuse them, he would take them to some little out-of-the-way bar, and the whole place would soon be swimming in champagne.

In answer, the Swede, who had a strong accent, said:

"If it's the Brown I'm thinking of, he once owned that big yacht over there, the last in the line: the *Pacific*. . . . But she has changed hands two or three times since then."

"Thank you."

The man and his two companions were at a loss to guess the reason for Maigret's visit. They watched him as he walked away, and he heard a suppressed giggle from the girls.

The only yacht in the harbor as big as the *Pacific* was the one that had been flying the Turkish flag. But, in contrast to the latter, the *Pacific* showed signs of neglect. There were rusty patches on the hull where the paint had flaked off, and all the brasswork was green.

A pathetic little sign was hanging from the side rail: FOR SALE.

Washed and neat in their tight-fitting uniforms, sailors were coming ashore from the yachts and wandering off in twos and threes toward the center of town.

When Maigret passed the *Ardena* on his way back, he was conscious of three pairs of eyes on him, and he felt sure there must be another pair peering at him from around some corner, where Yan had taken cover.

The streets were all lighted. Maigret had difficulty finding the garage again. There were one or two more questions he wanted to ask.

"What time last Friday did Brown come for his car?"

The mechanic had to be called.

"Ten to five," said the mechanic.

In other words, just enough time to get back to Cap d'Antibes at the hour they'd said.

"Was he alone? Nobody was waiting for him outside? . . . Did you notice anything wrong? He wasn't wounded?"

William Brown had left the Liberty Bar about two o'clock. What had he been doing between two and five?

There was nothing more for Maigret to do in Cannes. He waited for his bus, and then tucked himself into a corner and sat gazing idly at the headlights of the oncoming cars, which followed each other in procession along the main road.

The first person he saw as he got off in Place Macé was Inspector Boutigues, who was sitting on the terrace of the Café Glacier. Boutigues jumped up and ran to meet him.

"I've been looking for you ever since this morning. . . . Sit down. What'll you have? . . . Waiter! . . . Two Pernods."

"Not for me. I'll have a gentian," said Maigret, who wanted to know what it tasted like.

"First I questioned all the taxi drivers. Since none of them had taken you anywhere, I tried the bus conductors. That's how I knew you'd gone to Cannes."

He spoke quickly, eagerly. Maigret looked at him, surprised, but the little man went on:

"There are only five or six restaurants there where one can have a decent meal. I called them all. . . . Where the devil did you have lunch?"

Boutigues would have been astonished if Maigret had told him the truth, had told him about the wonderful leg of mutton and Jaja's salad flavored with garlic . . . about the glasses of whiskey . . . Sylvie. . . .

"The examining magistrate won't do anything without consulting you first. And now, I'll give you the news. The son has arrived."

"Whose son?"

Maigret grimaced. He had just swallowed a mouthful of gentian!

48

"Brown's son. He was in Amsterdam when . . ."

The trouble was that Maigret had a headache. He tried to concentate, but succeeded only with an effort.

"Brown has a son?"

"Several. Well, three. By his real wife, who lives in Australia . . . Only one of them is in Europe. He looks after the wool."

"The wool?"

At that moment Boutigues could hardly have had a very high opinion of the man who had come from Paris. But in fact, Maigret was still in the Liberty Bar. To be more precise, he was thinking about the waiter who played the horses, to whom Sylvie had spoken from the upstairs window.

"Yes. The Browns are the biggest wool people in Australia. They export to Europe. One of the sons looks after the sheep. Another, in Sydney, sees to the shipping. The third, here in Europe, travels from one port to another according to where the wool comes in—Liverpool, Havre, Hamburg, Amsterdam. . . . He's the one who . . ."

"And what does he say?"

"That his father must be buried as quickly as possible. He'll pay for everything. . . . He's in a hurry. Says he has to catch a plane tomorrow night."

"Is he in Antibes?"

"No. At Juan-les-Pins . . . He wanted a big hotel, where he could have a whole suite of rooms. He's arranged for his telephone line to Nice to be kept open all night, because he's expecting calls from Antwerp and Amsterdam, and I don't know where else."

"Has he been to the villa?"

"I suggested it, but he refused."

"What did he come for, then?"

"He's seen the examining magistrate. That's all. Merely says things must go quickly. And asks how much!"

"How much what?"

"How much it'll cost."

Maigret looked absently around Place Macé, while Boutigues continued:

"The magistrate waited for you in his office all afternoon. He couldn't very well refuse to allow the burial, now that the autopsy is finished. Brown's son telephoned three times, and finally he was told the funeral could take place first thing tomorrow morning."

"First thing in the morning?"

"To avoid having a crowd. . . . That's why I wanted to get hold of you. . . . They're closing the coffin this evening, so if you want to see the body . . ."

"No!"

That was quite definite. Maigret had no wish to see the corpse. He knew William Brown well enough without that.

There were a lot of people on the café terrace, and Boutigues noticed that eyes were turned toward the two of them. He rather liked it. Nevertheless, he whispered:

"We'd better lower our voices."

"Where's he to be buried?"

"Here . . . at the cemetery in Antibes. The hearse will be at the mortuary at seven. Everything's arranged. I mustn't forget to let Brown's son know the exact time."

"And the two women?"

"Nothing's been decided. . . . Perhaps the son would prefer . . ."

"Where did you say he was?"

"The Provençal in Juan-les-Pins. Do you want to see him?"

"Good-bye," said Maigret. "I'll see you at the funeral."

He was in a strange mood. He felt grim, yet at the same time he wanted to laugh. A taxi took him to the Provençal, where he was received by the doorman, passed on to a porter in gold-braided uniform, and finally ushered into the presence of a young man in a black suit sitting at a desk.

"Monsieur Brown? . . . I'll see if he's free. May I ask your name?"

Bells rang. Pageboys came and went. After about five minutes, Maigret was led along interminable corridors to a room marked Number 37. From behind the door came the sound of a typewriter and an irritable voice saying:

"Come in."

And Maigret found himself face to face with the son of William Brown, the third son, in charge of the department known as Wool–Europe.

His age was hard to tell. Perhaps thirty, perhaps forty. A tall, thin, clean-shaven man, whose face was already lined. Perfectly groomed, he wore a pearl tiepin in his black tie with narrow white stripes.

It would be impossible to imagine him untidy or spontaneous. Every hair was in place; every gesture, premeditated.

"You'll excuse me a moment? . . . Do sit down."

A typist was sitting at the Louis XV table. A secretary was speaking English into the telephone.

Brown's son finished dictating a cable in English, about some damages being claimed on account of a dockers' strike.

"Monsieur Brown, it's for you," said the secretary, handing him the telephone receiver.

"Hello! What is it? . . . Yes!"

He then listened for a long time without interrupting, and finally hung up after saying:

"No!"

He pressed an electric bell, asking Maigret:

"A glass of port?"

"No, thanks."

When the waiter came, he ordered it nonetheless.

He did everything calmly, but with an anxious air, as if the fate of the world depended on the most trivial of his actions—a nod of his head, a stroke of his pencil.

"Type that out in the next room, please."

And to his secretary: "Ask the examining magistrate . . ."

Finally he sat down with a sigh and crossed his legs.

"I'm afraid I'm tired. Are you handling this investigation?"

The waiter returned with the port, and pushed it over toward Maigret.

"It's an absurd affair, isn't it?"

"Not so absurd," Maigret said coldly.

"I mean annoying."

"Certainly. It's always annoying to get a knife between your shoulder blades and then to die."

Brown stood up, impatient. Opening the door to the next room, he gave some orders in English; then, coming back to Maigret, he held out his cigarette case.

"No, thanks. Nothing but a pipe."

Brown reached for a box of English tobacco that was standing on a little table.

"No, shag," said Maigret, pulling his little pouch from his pocket.

Brown paced the room with long strides.

"You know, perhaps, that my father led a . . . a rather wild life."

"He had a mistress."

"That's not all. Far from it. I'm sorry to have to say this, but if you don't understand, you may make . . . what do you call it? . . . a faux pas."

The telephone interrupted him. The secretary dashed in to

52

take it, answering this time in German, while Brown listened and signaled to him to say no. The call went on, however. Brown could stand it no longer, snatched the receiver from the secretary, and hung up.

"My father came to France many years ago, without my mother. . . . He nearly ruined us."

Brown couldn't keep still. While speaking, he shut the door behind the departing secretary. Returning, he pointed to the glass of port.

"You're not drinking?"

"No, thanks."

He waved impatiently.

"Well, my mother managed to take the business out of his hands. A guardian was named. . . . She suffered a lot. Worked very hard."

"It was she who put the business on its feet again?"

"With my uncle, yes."

"Her brother, I suppose?"

"Yes. My father had lost his sense of dignity . . . yes, dignity. . . . No need to go into detail. You understand?"

Maigret's eyes had been fixed on him steadily the whole time, and it seemed to throw the young man off stride. It was an oppressive look, and unfathomable.

"One question, Monsieur Brown—Monsieur Harry Brown, I believe, judging by the name on your luggage. Where were you last Friday?"

The answer did not come until the young man had paced the length of the room twice.

"What are you thinking?"

"Nothing. I simply asked you where you were."

"Is it important?"

"Perhaps yes; perhaps no."

"I was in Marseille, because the *Glasgow* was arriving. The ship carried a cargo of our wool, which is now being unloaded in Amsterdam, owing to the strike."

"You didn't see your father?"

"I didn't."

"One more question, the last. Who paid your father his allowance and how much was it?"

"I did. Five thousand francs a month . . . Perhaps you'd like to tell that to the newspapers?"

A typewriter could be heard through the door to the other room, especially the little bell at the end of each line and the thud of the carriage as it was slapped back.

Maigret stood up and reached for his hat.

"Thank you."

Brown was surprised.

"Is that all?"

"That's all. Thank you."

The telephone rang again, but the young man seemed not to notice it. He was staring incredulously at Maigret as the latter walked to the door.

Then, in some distress, he picked up an envelope from the table:

"I had this . . . I thought some police charity might like . . ."

Maigret was already out in the hallway. A moment later he was walking down the sumptuous staircase and across the lobby, conducted by a gold-braided lackey.

At nine o'clock, he was having dinner at the Hotel Bacon; at the same time, consulting the local telephone directory. As soon as he was finished, he called three numbers in Cannes, one after the other. On the third, the answer came:

"Yes. It's just across the street."

"Good! Would you be kind enough to tell Madame Jaja that the funeral is at seven tomorrow morning in Antibes. . . . Yes, the funeral . . . She'll understand."

He started pacing. Through a window he could see, a quarter of a mile away, the dead man's white villa, two windows of which were lighted.

No, he didn't feel up to that at all. Sleep was what he wanted.

"Is there a telephone at the Browns'?"

"Yes, Superintendent. Shall I call there?"

The neat little maid in a white cap, who reminded Maigret of a mouse, ran over to him.

"Monsieur, I have one of the women on the phone."

Maigret took the receiver.

"Hello! This is the superintendent. . . . Yes . . . I haven't been able to come over to see you. The funeral is at seven tomorrow morning. . . . What . . . No. Not this evening. I have some work to do. Good night, madame."

Doubtless the old woman was bustling off to tell her daughter. And then the two of them would hurry upstairs to get out their best black clothes, wondering if they would be ready in time.

The proprietress of the hotel came into the room, smiling sweetly.

"Did you like the bouillabaisse? . . . I had it made specially for you."

The bouillabaisse? Maigret searched his memory.

"Oh, yes. Delicious," he managed to say with a polite smile.

But he didn't remember it, not with Boutigues, the bus, the garage . . .

As for food, two things remained in his mind: Jaja's leg of mutton and the garlic-flavored salad.

And, from deeper down: the sickly smell of the port he hadn't drunk, and the no less sickly smell of Harry Brown's brilliantine.

"Bring me up a bottle of Vittel," he said as he turned to go upstairs.

CHAPTER FIVE

The Funeral

Though it was only just spring, the early-morning sun was quite strong. The streets were empty, and all the shutters were closed. The market, however, had come to life, the light, easygoing life of people who rise early and have a long day before them. They shouted from stall to stall, some in French, some in Italian.

Right in the middle of the market stood the town hall, which had a yellow façade and a double entrance at the top of some steps. In its basement was the morgue.

At ten to seven a hearse drew up, a distressing black thing among all the fruit and flowers. At the same time, Maigret arrived, and, a moment later, Boutigues, hurrying. He was still buttoning his waistcoat, having got up only ten minutes before.

"We have time for a drink," he said, pushing open the door of a little bar, where he ordered two glasses of rum.

"You know this has been very complicated. To start with, the son never said what price he wanted to pay for the coffin. I called him at the Provençal last evening. He said he didn't care, as long as it was of good quality. . . . Then the trouble began. There wasn't a single solid-oak coffin in Antibes, so I had to have one sent over from Cannes. It didn't get here till eleven o'clock. . . . Then, the service: I didn't know whether we ought to have it in church or not. I called the Provençal again, but they said he'd gone to bed. . . . So I simply had to do my best. . . . There you are!"

He pointed to a church a hundred yards away, whose doorway was draped with the conventional black curtains with silver fringe.

Maigret made no comment, though young Brown had certainly struck him as being more like a Protestant than a Catholic.

The bar, at the corner of a little street, had a door on the side as well as in front. As Maigret and Boutigues left by one door, a man entered by the other, and the superintendent caught his eye.

It was Joseph, the waiter at the casino in Cannes. He hesitated a moment, not knowing whether to acknowledge Maigret or not. Finally he decided on a vague nod.

Maigret guessed that he had brought Jaja and Sylvie to Antibes, and he was not mistaken. There they were, walking just in front of him toward the hearse. Jaja, panting for breath, was dragged along by the girl, who was apparently afraid of being late.

Sylvie had her blue suit on and looked quite the proper young woman. As for Jaja, she was obviously unused to walking. Very likely she had bad feet or swollen legs. She wore shiny black satin.

They must have got up at half past five to catch the first bus. A unique event in the Liberty Bar!

"Who are they?" asked Boutigues.

"I don't know," Maigret answered.

But at the same moment, the two women, having reached the hearse, stopped and turned around. And as soon as Jaja saw the superintendent, she bustled over to him.

"We aren't late? . . . Where is he?"

Sylvie had rings under her eyes, but showed the same hostile reserve toward Maigret as before.

"Joseph came with you?"

She was on the point of denying it, but decided not to.

"Who told you so?"

Boutigues stood to one side. Maigret saw a taxi which, unable to make its way through the market, stopped at a street corner.

The two women who got out created quite a stir. They were in deepest mourning; their heavy crepe veils almost touched the ground. They looked altogether incongruous in the sunshine and the busy, noisy crowd.

Maigret said to Jaja:

"Excuse me."

Boutigues was becoming anxious. He asked the undertaker to wait a few minutes longer before bringing out the coffin.

"We're not late?" asked the old woman. "It was the taxi, it didn't come at the right time."

She quickly spotted Jaja and Sylvie.

"Who are they?"

"I don't know."

"We don't want *them* butting in!"

Another taxi. The door opened before it had quite stopped, and out jumped Harry Brown, impeccably dressed in black, his light hair beautifully brushed, his face freshly shaved. His secretary was with him, also dressed in black, and carrying a wreath of local flowers.

At the same moment, Maigret noticed that Sylvie had vanished. Looking around, he saw her among the market stalls, standing by some baskets of flowers. When she returned, she had a huge bunch of Nice violets.

The two women in mourning were not to be outdone, and they too moved off, hurriedly, consulting one another. The old one fumbled in her purse while the other picked out a bunch of mimosa.

With a nod to Maigret and Boutigues, Brown took his place a few paces behind the hearse.

"I'd better tell him I've arranged for absolution," Boutigues said, sighing.

Around them in the market, activity subsided. People stood still to watch the spectacle. Twenty yards farther away, however, everything continued as usual: cries and laughter in a sea of flowers, fruit, and vegetables, in the sunshine, the smell of garlic, and the scent of mimosa.

Four men carried the large coffin, which was furnished with a profusion of bronze ornaments. Boutigues returned.

"He doesn't care. He just shrugged."

The crowd made way, and the horses stepped forward. Harry Brown advanced stiffly, hat in hand, looking at the toes of his polished shoes.

The four women hesitated, exchanging glances. Then, since neither pair yielded, they fell automatically into a single row behind Brown and his secretary.

The church doors were wide open. Inside, it was quite empty, and the coolness was delicious.

Brown waited at the top of the steps for the coffin to be lifted out of the hearse. He was used to ceremonies. To be

60

the center of attention caused him no embarrassment whatever. In fact, he calmly scrutinized the four women, though without showing undue curiosity.

Because the funeral had been arranged hurriedly, at the last minute, it was not surprising that the organist had been forgotten. The priest whispered to Boutigues in the sacristy. The latter was thoroughly put out when he rejoined Maigret.

"There'll be no music. We'd have to wait a quarter of an hour. . . . That is, if the organist's at home. He might be out mackerel fishing."

A few strangers entered the church, cast a look around, and went out again. And all the time Brown stood rigidly, but quite at ease, looking around with detached curiosity.

Without organ or choir, the service was soon over. The aspergillum sprinkled its holy water, and the four men carried out the coffin.

Outside, the day's heat had already begun. The cortege passed by a hairdresser's, where a man in a white coat was pulling down the shutters. Farther on, a man was shaving at an open window. Men and women, going to work, turned to stare at so incongruous a funeral—a mere handful of people following a sumptuous first-class coffin.

The two women from Cannes and the two from Antibes were still in a single row, though separated by a gap a yard wide. An empty taxi followed them.

Boutigues, who had all the responsibilities on his shoulders, was nervous.

"I hope there won't be a scene," he said.

There was none. The cemetery, with all its flowers, was almost as gay as the market. The priest was there already, standing beside the open grave with the little choirboy who carried the holy water.

Brown was invited to throw in the first handful of earth.

There was a moment's hesitation over who should be next. Then the old woman in mourning pushed her daughter forward and followed her.

Brown, with long strides, had already reached the cemetery gate, where the taxi was waiting. Maigret and Boutigues were still by the grave, standing a little to one side.

Another hesitation. Jaja and Sylvie did not want to leave without saying good-bye. But the other women cut in front. Gina wept, squeezing her handkerchief into a ball under her veil and dabbing her eyes.

With an air of mistrust, the mother asked:

"That's his son, isn't it? . . . I suppose he'll be wanting to come to the house."

"He may, but I don't know."

"Are you coming today?"

She was speaking to Maigret, but her eyes were on Jaja and Sylvia, who had all her attention.

"Where did *they* come from? . . . Creatures like that shouldn't have been allowed . . ."

Birds were singing in every tree. The gravediggers were busy, and shovelfuls of earth fell in a steady rhythm, the sound becoming gradually fainter as the grave filled. Sylvie stood staring, her lips pale. The wreath and the other flowers had been put on the neighboring grave for the time being.

Jaja waited impatiently for the others to go, so she could speak to Maigret. She was hot and kept wiping her face. And she had been on her feet long enough.

"Yes," said Maigret to Gina's mother. "I'll be coming along soon."

The black veils withdrew toward the gate. Jaja approached with a sigh of relief.

"So they're the ones! . . . Was he really married?"

Sylvie was still standing with her eyes on the grave, which was almost filled in.

It was now Boutigues' turn to be impatient. He didn't dare go up and listen to the conversation.

"Is the son paying for that coffin?"

Jaja was visibly ill at ease.

"A funny funeral," she went on. "I don't know why, but I'd never have thought it would be like that. . . . I couldn't have cried if I wanted. . . ."

Only now were her feelings coming to the surface. She looked around the cemetery disconsolately.

"It wasn't even sad. . . . One might have thought . . ."

"One might have thought what?"

"I don't know. . . . It's as if it wasn't a real funeral."

She stifled a sob, dabbed her eyes, and turned to Sylvie.

"Come. Joseph's waiting."

The gatekeeper, on the doorstep of the cemetery lodge, was cutting up an eel.

"Well, what do you think?"

Boutigues was worried. He was confused and felt that things were not going right.

Maigret lighted his pipe.

"I think that William Brown was murdered," was all he answered.

"Certainly."

They walked through streets where the awnings were already lowered over the shop windows. The barber they had passed before now sat outside his door reading his paper. In Place Macé, the two women from Cannes were standing with Joseph, waiting for their bus.

"Let's sit down and have a drink," suggested Boutigues.

Maigret didn't refuse. An overwhelming lassitude had taken hold of him. A succession of confused images passed through his mind, and he made no attempt to sort them out.

On the terrace of the Glacier, he sat with his eyes half shut against the glare of the sun. His overlapping lashes made a shadowy curtain, through which objects and people looked dreamlike.

He watched Joseph hoist Fat Jaja into the bus. Then a dapper little man in white, wearing a sun helmet, slowly walked by, leading a purple-tongued chow.

Superimposed upon these real images were others: an unshaven William Brown at the wheel of an old car, driving his two women from shop to shop, with the collar of his nightshirt showing.

His son, Harry, would now be back in his grand suite at the Provençal, dictating cables, telephoning, and pacing up and down with long, regular strides.

"A strange business," sighed Boutigues, who did not care for long silences.

He uncrossed his legs and crossed them the other way before adding:

"It's too bad we forgot about the organist."

"William Brown was murdered."

It was for his own benefit that Maigret repeated the words. He was trying to convince himself that, after all, something serious had occurred. His collar was too tight, and his forehead glistened with perspiration. He gazed with longing at the lump of ice that floated in his glass.

Brown was murdered. . . . He left home, as he did every month, and drove to Cannes. Leaving the car at the garage, he went to the bank or wherever it was his son sent his allowance. Then he spent a week at the Liberty Bar.

A week of warm laziness like that which had now overcome Maigret. A week in slippers, shifting from one chair to another, eating and drinking with Jaja and watching Sylvie coming and going half-naked . . .

On Friday afternoon at two, he left. At ten to five he retrieved the car, and a quarter of an hour later he reached the villa, wounded, and fell dead on the front steps, while Gina, thinking him drunk, scolded from an upstairs window. . . . He had the usual two thousand francs on him.

These thoughts floated through Maigret's brain as he watched the passers-by or the lump of ice in his glass through the curtain of his eyelashes.

Boutigues muttered:

"I can't imagine who had the slightest interest in his death."

That, of course, was the question.

Brown's two women, for instance? No, they had every reason to keep him alive as long as possible, since, out of the two thousand francs he brought home every month, they always managed to save some.

The two in Cannes? They had nothing to gain and everything to lose. Wasn't Brown one of the few customers of the Liberty Bar, and one who kept the whole household in food and drink when he stayed each month? Didn't he sometimes pay Jaja's electricity and gas bills? Didn't he pay for Sylvie's silk stockings?

The only one who stood to gain anything was Harry Brown—or, rather, the Brown family—who would no longer have to pay the father five thousand francs a month.

But what were five thousand francs a month to people who sold wool by the shipload?

Boutigues sighed again.

"I'll end up by thinking, like the public, that it's a spy case."

"Waiter," called Maigret, "the same again."

He regretted it instantly. He wanted to cancel the order, but it would look silly. It would be a confession of his weakness.

For years he would remember this hour spent on the terrace of the Café Glacier on Place Macé in Antibes. . . . It was one of his rare moments of weakness, of surrender.

Certainly the surroundings did not help. The air was soft and warm. A young girl was selling mimosa on the corner. She was barefoot, and her legs were bronzed by the sun.

A gray sports car with chromium trim slid past toward the sea. In it were three girls in beach outfits and, at the wheel, a young Romeo with a thin mustache.

It was too much like a vacation. That had been the trouble from the start. It had been the same the evening before in Cannes—the harbor at sunset, and, especially, the *Ardena* and its owner, showing off in front of two girls whose dresses revealed their figures.

Maigret was dressed in black, exactly as he always was in Paris. His bowler was altogether out of place here.

There was a poster with blue letters in front of him:

CASINO OF JUAN-LES-PINS
GRAND GALA! FIREWORKS!

And the lump of ice slowly melted in his milky-green glass.

Vacations! To lean over the side of a green or orange boat and stare at the bottom, at the moving, mottled light caused by the ripples above . . . To lie down under a parasol pine and listen to the buzzing of a bumblebee . . .

Above all, not to worry about a man he hadn't known a week before, who had had the misfortune to get a knife stuck in his back!

Or about those women, whose faces haunted him, as if it were he who had slept with them. What were they to him?

66

Some superintendent of the Police Judiciare!

A smell of melting tar drifted over Place Macé. Boutigues had bought another red carnation and was sticking it into his buttonhole.

And William Brown? He was buried, wasn't he? What more could he want? . . . Why should Maigret bother about him any longer? *He* never owned one of the biggest yachts in Europe. *He* hadn't got mixed up with those two Martinis—the old one with the painted face and the young one with the big rear. . . . *He* hadn't sunk deep in the slovenly oblivion of the Liberty Bar.

Little puffs of warm air caressed his face. More vacationers passed. Everybody seemed to be on vacation here. Even Boutigues, who couldn't keep silent and who now murmured:

"Anyhow, I'm glad they didn't leave me the responsibility of . . ."

Maigret stopped looking at the world through his eyelashes and turned to his companion. He was rather red in the face from the heat and his two drinks. His eyes looked sleepy, but after a second or two they were back to normal.

"That's right!" he said, getting up. "Waiter! How much?"

"Leave it to me."

"Nothing of the kind." And Maigret threw some money on the table.

Yes, it was an hour he would remember. He had actually been tempted to do nothing, to let things slide, as many others would have done. . . .

And the day was so glorious.

"Are you going? . . . Do you have an idea?"

No. His head was much too full of sunshine for ideas. But, since he did not want to discuss it, he merely muttered:

"William Brown was murdered."

Though to himself he added:

67

And what the hell does it matter to anybody?

What did it matter to all these people who basked in the sun like lizards during the day and then went to the gala with fireworks in the evening?

"I have some work to do," he said, holding out his hand to Boutigues.

He slowly walked off, then stopped to allow a car to pass— a car that might have cost up to three hundred thousand francs. It was driven by a girl of about eighteen, who looked straight in front of her with a frown.

"Brown was murdered." He repeated the words over and over again.

He was beginning to realize that the lure of the Riviera was not to be underestimated. He turned his back to the Café Glacier and, to make sure of no backsliding, started giving himself orders, just as if he were speaking to a subordinate:

"Find out what Brown was doing between two and ten of five last Friday."

For that, he'd have to go to Cannes. And for that, he'd have to take the bus.

So there he stood, under a street lamp, waiting for it, his hands in his pockets, his pipe between his teeth, and a look on his face that was none too agreeable.

CHAPTER SIX

A *Round of Hotels*

In Cannes, Maigret plodded around for hours doing the dreary work usually given to inspectors. But he needed to act, or at least to create the illusion of action.

From the police Vice Squad, he learned that Sylvie was in their records, and was well-known.

"I've never had any trouble with her," said the sergeant who covered her district. "She behaves herself, and comes pretty regularly for inspection."

"And the Liberty Bar?"

"So you've heard of it? A funny place. It kept us guessing a long time, and keeps a lot of people guessing still. Hardly a month goes by that we don't get an anonymous letter about it. . . . At first we thought Fat Jaja might be dealing in drugs. We kept her under observation. But I can assure you there's nothing of that kind. . . . Then people hinted that it was a haunt for perverts."

"I know that's not the case," said Maigret.

"No. It's really quite harmless. Old Mother Jaja has an irresistible attraction for a certain type: older men, who no longer care for anything but simply like to sit and tipple with her. . . . Besides the bar, she has a small pension, because her husband died accidentally."

"I know."

In another department, Maigret asked about Joseph.

"We keep an eye on him, because he's always at the races. But nothing has ever been brought up against him."

No leads. Hands in his pockets, Maigret strode through the town with an increasingly disgruntled look.

He began to visit the big hotels, where he examined the registers. After stopping to have lunch in a restaurant near the station, he went on. By three o'clock he was reasonably sure that Harry Brown had not spent the previous Tuesday or Wednesday night in Cannes, or Thursday or Friday either.

It was ridiculous—doing things just to keep busy.

Young Brown could just as well have driven over from Marseille and gone back the same day.

Maigret returned to the Vice Squad and borrowed the photograph they had of Sylvie. He already had one of Wiliam Brown, which he'd taken from the villa.

And he plunged into a new milieu: little hotels, particularly those around the harbor, where you could take a room, not only for the night, but also by the hour.

The proprietors of these places knew immediately that he belonged to the police. It was their business to, since they were afraid of the police more than anything.

"Wait a moment. I'll ask the chambermaid."

There would be hurried footsteps on dark staircases. This was a world where you didn't have to probe deep to find the seamy side of life.

"That big man? No, I don't think I've ever seen him here."

It was the photograph of William Brown that Maigret showed first, after which he would produce Sylvie's.

Hers was recognized almost every time.

"Yes, she's been here. But we haven't seen her lately."

"At night?"

"No, not particularly. When she comes with somebody, it's always 'for a moment.' "

Hotel Bellevue . . . Hotel du Port . . . Hotel Bristol . . . Hotel d'Auvergne . . .

And many more, most of them on little streets, most of them discreet, too, so that you wouldn't know they were hotels at all if it wasn't for the open corridor and the sign at the entrance: RUNNING WATER. MODERATE PRICES.

Sometimes Maigret would strike a somewhat better place with a carpet on the stairs. In others he would meet a furtive couple in the hall who looked the other way.

And again and again he'd find himself facing the harbor, where six-meter racing boats had been hauled up on slips. Sailors were painting them with care, while groups of idlers stood watching.

In Paris, they had talked about "tactful handling," but it didn't look as though tact would be needed. If things went on like this, there would be nothing to be tactful about.

He smoked pipe after pipe, filling a fresh one before the other was finished. He always carried two or three with him.

He was fed up with Cannes—furious with a woman who persisted in trying to sell him some shellfish, and then with a barefoot boy who nearly tripped him and then laughed in his face.

"Do you know this man?"

For the twentieth time, he held out William Brown's photograph.

"He's never come here."

"And this woman?"

"Sylvie? . . . She's upstairs."

"Alone?"

The landlord shrugged, and called:

"Albert! . . . Come down a minute."

The man came down. He was dirty, and he looked sideways at the superintendent.

"Is Sylvie still upstairs?"

"In Number 7."

"Have they ordered drinks?"

"Nothing at all."

"Then they won't be long," said the landlord to Maigret. "If you want to speak to her, just wait."

It was called the Hotel Beauséjour, and was on a street running parallel to the harbor, opposite a baker's.

Did Maigret want to see Sylvie again? Had he anything to ask her if he did?

He really didn't know. He was tired. But by now his attitude had something predatory about it, as if he was hot on the trail.

Anyhow, he wouldn't wait in front of the hotel, because the baker's wife opposite was looking at him mockingly through her shop window.

Was Sylvie in such demand that people waited in line for her favors? It made Maigret furious to think he was being taken for one of her clients.

He strolled to the corner, intending to walk around the block to fill the time. When he reached the quay, he turned to study a taxi that had pulled up to the curb; the driver was pacing on the sidewalk.

Something struck him, but he couldn't tell what it was. He looked away, but his eyes were drawn back. It was not the taxi itself, but the driver, who somehow recalled . . . Yes! He had it! The funeral that morning . . .

"You're from Antibes, aren't you?"

"From Juan-les-Pins."

"And you followed a funeral this morning, to the cemetery."

"Yes. Why?"

"Who's your fare here? The same person?"

The driver looked his questioner over from head to foot.

"What do you want to know for?"

"I'm the police—I want to know!"

"All right. It's the same one. He's hired me by the day. Since lunchtime yesterday."

"Where is he now?"

"I don't know. He went off that way."

The driver pointed to a street, then suddenly asked anxiously:

"You're not going to arrest him before he pays me, are you?"

Maigret stood quite still, forgetting to smoke, and stared at the taxi's old-fashioned hood. Then he thought that the couple in the hotel might have left, and he hurried back there.

The baker's wife saw him coming and called her husband from the back. A moment later, a floury face joined hers at the window.

Well, Maigret no longer cared. His thoughts were focused on room Number 7. Looking up at the hotel, he wondered which window belonged to it.

He was trying not to crow too soon.

And yet . . . No, it couldn't be a coincidence. This was the first time that two links had actually come together to make the beginning of a chain.

Sylvie and Harry Brown meeting in a disreputable hotel!

Twenty times he walked from the Beauséjour to the corner of the little street leading to the quay. Twenty times he saw the taxi standing in the same place. As for the driver, he had taken up a position on the corner, to be able to see what happened.

At last someone opened the glass-paneled door. Sylvie stepped briskly into the street and almost bumped into Maigret.

"Good afternoon," he said.

She stopped dead. He had never seen her so pale, and when she opened her mouth, she was unable to utter a sound.

"Your friend's dressing?"

She looked around wildly, and even dropped her bag. When Maigret picked it up, she snatched it from his hand as if terrified he would open it.

"One moment."

"Excuse me . . . Someone's expecting me. . . . Do you mind if we walk?"

"That's just what I don't want to do, particularly in that direction."

She was more touching than pretty. Her huge eyes seemed to swallow up the rest of her face. In an agony of dismay, she almost panted.

"What do you want with me?"

She looked as though she was about to run. To prevent anything of the kind, Maigret took her hand, holding it in such a way that the baker and his wife could easily take it for an affectionate gesture.

"Is Harry still there?"

"I don't understand."

"Very well. We'll wait for him together. . . . And be careful, child. No nonsense! . . . And leave that bag alone."

Maigret took it out of her hand. Through the silky material he could feel something that suggested a wad of money.

"We don't want a scene! There are people watching."

And passers-by. They probably thought Maigret and Sylvie were arguing over how much.

"Please! Please!"

"No."

And then he added in a whisper:

"Calm down, or I'll put you in handcuffs."

She looked at him, her pupils dilated with fear, and then, resigned or broken, she hung her head.

"Harry seems to be in no hurry to come down."

She made no attempt to persuade him he was wrong. She said nothing.

"Did you know him before?"

They were standing right in the sun. Sylvie's face was covered with sweat. She appeared to be groping desperately for an inspiration that she couldn't find.

"Listen . . ."

"I'm listening."

But no. She changed her mind and said nothing. She bit her lip.

"Is Joseph waiting for you somewhere?"

"Joseph?"

She was distracted, panicky. And all at once they heard steps in the hotel. Sylvie trembled and dared not look down the dark corridor.

The steps changed their note as they advanced along the tiled passage. The glass-paneled door opened, then quickly closed again. Silence.

They could not see Harry Brown in the shadow, but surely he had seen them. The pause was brief, however. The door opened a second time, and he emerged into the sunshine. He showed no embarrassment. Without the least hesitation, he walked past, giving Maigret a casual nod.

Maigret still held Sylvie's unresisting hand. To catch Brown, he would have had to let her go. A ridiculous scene to play in front of the baker and his wife!

"Come with me," he said.

"Are you arresting me?"

"Don't worry about that."

He had to telephone at once, but nothing would induce him to let go of Sylvie. There were some cafés in the neighborhood. He entered the first he came to and dragged her with him right into the telephone booth.

A moment or two later he was speaking to Inspector Boutigues.

"Go as quickly as you can to the Hotel Provençal. Ask for Harry Brown and tell him politely but firmly not to leave Antibes until I've seen him. If necessary, stop him!"

Sylvie listened limply. There was no fight left in her, no spark of rebellion.

"What would you like to drink?" he asked, sitting her down at a table.

"It's all the same to me."

She was carrying her bag now, but Maigret kept an eye on it. The waiter looked at them inquisitively, sensing something unusual. A little girl was going from table to table selling violets. Maigret took the bunch she offered and presented it to Sylvie. He groped in his pockets for money, his face clouding. Suddenly, when it was least expected, he seized Sylvie's bag, saying:

"You don't mind, do you? . . . I don't have any change."

It was done so quickly and so naturally that she had no time to protest. Her fingers clenched slightly, but not until the bag was out of her grasp.

The little girl waited gravely, selecting another bunch from her basket. Maigret was looking under a fat bundle of thousand-franc notes for some small coins.

"And now let's go," he said, standing up.

He was somewhat nervous himself and longed to get away from the eyes of the curious.

"Shall we pay a call on good Mother Jaja?"

Sylvie followed obediently. She was beaten. And as they walked along they looked like any other couple, except that the gentleman was carrying the lady's bag.

"You go first."

She went down the two steps into the bar, and then walked over to the other door. Through its muslin curtain, a man's back was visible as he jumped abruptly from his seat.

It was Yan, the Swedish steward, who blushed to the roots of his hair upon seeing Maigret.

"You again? . . . Look, my friend, do me the favor of taking a walk."

Jaja didn't understand but she could see from Sylvie's face that something had happened. So she asked the steward:

"Come tomorrow, Yan, will you?"

"I don't know."

Cap in hand, and disconcerted by the superintendent's intense stare, he did not know how to take his leave.

"Yes," said Maigret. "Go. Good-bye." And he opened the door for the steward and shut it again behind him.

He gave a sharp turn to the key, then said to Sylvie:

"You can take your hat off."

In a timid voice Jaja ventured:

"So you met? . . ."

"We met."

The air was so charged that she didn't even offer him a drink. To regain her composure, she picked a newspaper up from the floor and folded it. Then she went to the stove and looked at something cooking there.

Maigret filled his pipe slowly and carefully. He, too, went to the stove, where he rolled a piece of newspaper into a spill and lit it from the fire.

Sylvie remained standing by the table. She had removed her hat and put it down in front of her.

Maigret sat, opened her bag, and started counting the money, laying the bills one after the other in a pile among the dirty glasses on the table.

". . . eighteen . . . nineteen . . . twenty," he counted. "Twenty thousand francs."

At the sound of his counting, Jaja spun around. Bewildered, she looked at the notes, then at Sylvie, then at the superintendent. She was trying hard to understand.

"What's this?"

"Nothing extraordinary," growled Maigret. "Sylvie caught a bigger fish than usual today. That's all. And what do you think his name was? . . . Harry Brown!"

He had made himself quite at home. His elbows were on the table, his pipe in his mouth, his bowler shoved to the back of his head.

Twenty thousand francs "for a moment," as they say at the Hotel Beauséjour.

To cover her confusion, Jaja wiped her fat hands on her apron. She couldn't find a word to say. She was dumbfounded.

Deathly pale, Sylvie looked at neither of them. She gazed into space, waiting for the next blow to fall.

"You can sit down," said Maigret sharply.

She obeyed mechanically.

"You, too, Jaja . . . Wait! . . . Bring some clean glasses."

Sylvie was sitting in the same place as the day before, when she ate in her dressing gown, her bare breast inches from him.

Jaja put a bottle and glasses on the table and sat down on the edge of her chair.

"And now, my children," said Maigret, "I'm listening."

The smoke from his pipe drifted slowly toward the little blue window, which the sun no longer reached. Jaja looked at Sylvie.

The girl, whether from obstinacy or because her thoughts were far away, looked at nothing, said nothing.

"I'm waiting."

But it was no good. He could have repeated it a hundred times; he could have waited ten years. Only Jaja, her chin sinking into her bosom, sighed and said:

"My God! . . . If I'd thought . . ."

As for Maigret, he could hardly contain himself. He got up and paced.

"She'll have to . . ." he muttered.

But she just sat there, lifeless, staring. He was on the verge of losing his temper. Twice, three times he passed close to Sylvie.

"I have time. . . . But . . ."

The fourth time, he could stand it no longer. It was automatic. His hand seized the girl's shoulder, without realizing the force of his grip.

She lifted her arm as though to ward off a blow, like a little girl who fears a beating.

"Well?"

She broke down from the pain. Bursting into sobs, she cried out:

"Brute! . . . Dirty bute! . . . I'll tell you nothing . . . nothing! . . ."

Jaja was miserable. Maigret, frowning, sank into his chair.

And Sylvie continued crying, without hiding her face or wiping away her tears, but she was crying from anger more than from pain.

The door of the bar opened, and a customer came in, an event that hardly happened once a day. He leaned an elbow on the counter and began fiddling with the slot machine.

CHAPTER SEVEN

The Will

With a scowl, Maigret rose from his chair. He was anxious to intercept any move by either of the two women. Suppose, for instance, the customer was really an emissary from Joseph? He quickly unlocked the door and went into the bar.

"What do you want?"

The man was so taken aback that the superintendent, in spite of his foul mood, nearly laughed out loud. He was a seedy, dull, graying, middle-aged man, who had no doubt slunk around to the Liberty Bar by back streets, with erotic visions in his mind. But instead of Jaja or Sylvie, it was Maigret at his gruffest who came to serve him.

"A beer," he stammered, letting go of the slot-machine handle.

Through the muslin curtains, the superintendent could see the two women. Jaja, now standing behind the girl, was asking questions, and Sylvie answered dully.

"There isn't any beer."

That is, Maigret couldn't see any near at hand.

"Then give me anything you want. . . . Some port . . ."

Maigret picked up a bottle at random and poured some of it into the first glass he found. The man took a gulp and hastened to say:

"How much?"

"Two francs."

Maigret glanced from time to time into the room behind, where Jaja had sat down again, and at the bar across the street, in which he could hardly make out the moving figures.

His customer slouched off, bewildered, and Maigret returned to the other room and sat down astride his chair.

Jaja's attitude was slightly different. She had been anxious before, being unaware of what the trouble was. Now her anxiety had taken shape. She looked thoughtfully at Sylvie—with pity certainly, but also with a touch of reproach. A look that seemed to say:

"A fine mess you've got yourself into! And it won't be easy to get out of it."

She began cautiously:

"You know, Superintendent, men are strange creatures . . ."

Lame words. She was conscious of this, and Sylvie was too. Nevertheless, Jaja labored on:

"He saw her this morning at the funeral and took a fancy to her. . . . He's so rich that . . ."

Maigret sighed, filled another pipe, and gazed gloomily at the window. A mournful atmosphere filled the room.

Jaja decided to hold her tongue, for fear of making matters worse. Sylvie was no longer crying. Motionless, she waited for whatever was to come.

Only the alarm clock went busily on with the day's work,

pushing its black hands, which seemed too heavy for it, around its pasty face.

Ticktock, ticktock, ticktock . . .

The sound seemed to fill the room. It was almost unbearably loud. A white cat in the back yard came and sat outside the window.

Ticktock, ticktock, ticktock . . .

Jaja, who wasn't made for tense situations, got up and fetched a bottle of whiskey from the kitchen cupboard. Pouring three glasses, as if nothing were wrong, she pushed one over to Maigret without a word, and another to Sylvie.

The twenty thousand francs still lay on the table beside Sylvie's open bag.

Ticktock, ticktock, ticktock . . .

For the next hour and a half there was silence, except for the ticking and an occasional sigh from Jaja, whose eyes got brighter and brighter as she drank.

Sometimes there was the noise of children playing in the alley. Other times, the bell of a distant streetcar could be heard. And once the door of the bar opened, and an arab stuck his head in, calling out:

"Peanuts! Peanuts!"

He waited a moment, but when there was no response, he shut the door again and moved on.

It was six o'clock when the door opened again. This time there was a faint stir in the kitchen, which told Maigret that it was what they were expecting. Jaja started to get up, but a look from him was enough to keep her in her place. Sylvie, to show indifference, turned her head away.

The kitchen door opened, and Joseph came in. The first thing he saw was Maigret's back, then the table, the glasses, the bottles, the open bag, the money.

The superintendent slowly turned around, and the newcomer, motionless, could find only one word to utter:

"Shit!"

"Shut the door . . . Have a seat . . ."

The waiter closed the door, but remained standing. He frowned and looked defiant, but did not lose his presence of mind.

Self-possessed, he went to Jaja and kissed her on the forehead.

"Good afternoon."

He did the same to Sylvie, who did not even raise her head.

"What's the matter?"

At that moment, Maigret realized that he had hold of the wrong end of the stick. But, as always in such a case, he gripped it all the tighter.

"Where do you come from?"

"Guess."

Joseph took out his wallet and from it produced a card. It was an identity card, the kind all foreign residents in France carried.

"I was late. . . . I've been to the prefecture to get it renewed."

The date stamped on the outside confirmed this. Opening it, Maigret read: "Joseph Ambrosini; born, Milan; profession, waiter."

"You haven't been to see Harry Brown?"

"Me?"

"And you didn't see him on Tuesday or Wednesday last week?"

Joseph looked at him with a smile, as much as to say:

"What are you babbling about?"

"Look here, Ambrosini! You're Sylvie's lover, aren't you?"

"It's to find that out you came here? My God!"

"Come, come! You're what is politely called her protector."

Poor Jaja! She had never been so miserable in her life. She had drunk so much, she couldn't see straight. Now and then she opened her mouth to put in a placating word. It was obvious what she wanted to say:

"Now, now, children! Why don't you shake hands and be friends? Life's too short for arguing. Let's have a drink together and forget all about this."

As for Joseph, it was obvious that this was not his first brush with the law. He kept his head, he didn't try to be too clever.

"You have been misinformed," was all he said.

"So you don't know where these twenty thousand francs came from?"

"I assume Sylvie earned them. . . . She's pretty enough for—"

"That'll do!"

Maigret was on his feet again, pacing up and down the little room. Sylvie looked at her feet, but Joseph was ready to look anybody in the face.

"Have a drop of this," Jaja said to him, taking the opportunity to fill her own glass.

Maigret spent some time making up his mind. He stood facing the alarm clock, whose hands were now at quarter past six. When he turned around, it was to say:

"The two of you will come with me. I am arresting you both."

Joseph did not wince. With a touch of sarcasm he muttered: "As you wish."

The superintendent put the money in his pocket. Then, after handing Sylvie her hat and bag, he turned to Joseph.

"Handcuffs? Or will you give me your word you won't . . . ?"

"We'll go with you."

Sobbing, Jaja threw her arms around Sylvie, who had trouble freeing herself. In fact, they all had a hard time keeping her from following them down the street.

Lights were being turned on. It was again evening. They passed near the street where the Hotel Beauséjour stood, but Joseph didn't so much as glance at it.

At the police station, the day men were strolling off. The sergeant hurriedly gave Maigret the necessary papers to sign.

"Lock them up separately . . . I'll probably come to see them tomorrow."

Sylvie had sat down on a bench. Joseph started rolling a cigarette, but a guard did not allow him to finish.

Maigret left without a word to them. At the door he turned to look at Sylvie. She was staring at the ground. Finally, with a shrug he walked out, muttering:

"Too bad!"

Wedged in a corner of the bus, he did not notice as it filled to overflowing, that an old lady was standing right beside him. Looking out the window, he wached the headlights of passing cards, and, quite oblivious, puffed furiously at his pipe, until the old lady cleared her throat and said:

"Excuse me, monsieur."

The words brought him back to earth. He sprang to his feet, did not know where to knock his pipe out, and presented such a picture of apologetic confusion that a young couple behind him burst out laughing.

At half past seven he pushed his way through the revolving doors of the Provençal, and found Inspector Boutigues talking to the manager from one of the easy chairs in the lobby.

"Well?"

"He's upstairs," answered Boutigues, who looked worried.

"You told him what I said?"

"Yes. He didn't seem surprised at all. I was expecting him to make a fuss."

The manager was waiting for an opportunity to put a word in; as soon as he opened his mouth, however, Maigret made for the elevator.

"Shall I wait for you?" cried Boutigues.

"If you like."

He was only too familiar with the state of mind he had been in for the last few hours. It made him furious. It always did, and that never helped matters.

It was the feeling that he'd made a mistake, that everything was wrong. He'd had it from the moment he met Sylvie at the hotel door. . . . He had shut his eyes to it, or tried to, and simply pushed ahead.

That's how it always was. If he felt he was getting into a mess, he became so determined to prove himself right that he waded in all the deeper.

The elevator carried him up in a slither of well-greased steel.

" . . . a case that needs tactful handling and no trouble."

That's what he'd been sent to Antibes for. So there would be no awkward revelations, no scandal.

At any other time, he would have entered Brown's suite without his pipe. This time he lighted it deliberately. He knocked, and, without waiting, barged in.

The scene he found was almost identical with the one the day before. Brown, perfectly groomed, was giving orders to his secretary, answering the telephone, and dictating a cable to Sydney.

"Excuse me a moment, will you?" he said.

No trace of anxiety. This man was at ease in every circumstance! Had he faltered, that morning, at his father's funeral, because of the presence of those four women? No.

And this afternoon, when he left that disreputable hotel, had he hesitated? Only for a second.

Brown continued dictating. At the same time, he picked up a box of cigars, placed it on a little table by Maigret and rang a bell.

"That's all, James. You can take the phone into the next room."

And when the waiter appeared:

"A whiskey, please."

How much of it was real? How much of it acting?

A matter of education, thought Maigret. He must have gone to Oxford or Cambridge.

That was an old grudge of his—the resentment of a pupil of the Lycée Stanislas. A resentment, however, that was not unmixed with admiration.

"You can take the typewriter into the next room, too, mademoiselle."

But seeing her encumbered with a fat notebook and pencils, Brown picked the heavy thing up himself and carried it into the next room.

He said nothing until the waiter had poured Maigret a glass of whiskey and left the room. Then he took out his wallet and from it pulled a stamped document. He handed it to the superintendent.

"Read this . . . You understand English?"

"Badly."

"This is what I bought for twenty thousand francs at the Hotel Beauséjour today."

He sat down. The action was like a relaxation.

"I must, first of all, explain a few things to you. . . . You

don't know Australia, do you? It's a pity. My father, before
his marriage, owned a very large estate. As large as one of the
departments of France. After his marriage, because my mother
brought with her an estate that was not much smaller, he
became the biggest sheepman in the country."

Brown spoke slowly, taking pains to make himself clear, yet
without wasting words.

"Are you a Protestant?" asked Maigret.

"We all are, on both sides of the family."

He started to go on, but Maigret interrupted him:

"Your father was not educated in Europe, was he?"

"No. That wasn't done so much in those days. . . . He
came here only after his marriage. Five years after, when he
already had three children."

In his mind's eye, Maigret reconstructed the whole picture.
Perhaps it wasn't correct in every detail, but he felt sure he
was right in the essentials.

He imagined a huge foursquare house standing in the middle of a vast estate and inhabited by serious people who looked
like Presbyterian ministers.

William Brown succeeds his father, marries, has children,
and occupies himself with his work. . . .

"One day he came to Europe, because of a lawsuit."

"Alone?"

"He came alone."

How obvious it was! Paris, London, Berlin. The Côte d'Azur.
William Brown suddenly sees that, with his colossal fortune,
he can be almost a king in this brilliant world full of seductions.

"And he never went back?" asked Maigret.

"No. . . ." The lawsuit dragged on. People in the wool
business, whom he met, took him around, introduced him to
high life, low life, women. . . .

"For two years he postponed his return."

"Who looked after things at home?"

"My mother . . . And her brother . . . She felt obliged to, since she had received letters telling her . . ."

Maigret could see it all too clearly. Brown, who had known only land, sheep, pastures, and the next house, had kicked over the traces and plunged into all the unknown pleasures.

He put off his return, then put it off again. He let the lawsuit drag on, and when it did get settled, he found other excuses to stay.

He bought a yacht and entertained guests by the dozen—smart people, rich people, people who could afford to laugh at every social convention.

"So your mother and your uncle succeeded in placing him under an official guardian?"

"Well, that's what you do in France. Things are a bit different with us. Put it this way: we took the business out of his hands."

How did they manage it? Was it done legally or illegally? In any case, one fine day William Brown must have awakened in Nice or Monte Carlo to find that he was no longer a rich Australian sheepman, but a poor relation living on an allowance.

"For a long time, he continued to live on credit, and we paid his debts," Brown said.

"And then you stopped paying?"

"No. I continued to deposit, in a bank in Cannes, an allowance of five thousand francs a month."

Maigret felt that something remained unsaid. Suddenly he asked:

"Did you come to propose something else to your father, shortly before his death?"

It was in vain that he watched the Australian for signs of nervousness. With perfect composure, Brown answered:

"Let me explain. The situation between my father and the family was never really cleared up. For fifteen years he has been fighting for what he claims are his rights. It's been a big lawsuit. Five lawyers have been working solely on that. And, pending a final settlement, we have been under an injunction not to dispose of any of the property. It tied our hands, and more than once prevented us from doing some very good business."

"There are lawyers in Australia defending your father's interests?"

"Shady lawyers."

"Of course! And against him are your mother, your uncle, your brothers, and you?"

"Yes."

"And what were you offering him to disappear completely?"

"A million."

"He would have been better off with that than with his allowance. . . . Why did he refuse?"

"To annoy us. It became an obsession with him. He was absolutely determined not to leave us in peace."

"Then he refused . . ."

"Not only that. He also said that he had taken steps to ensure that our troubles would continue if he died."

"What troubles?"

"The lawsuit. It's not so much the cost: it's been doing us a lot of harm."

Yes. The explanations it would require . . . There was the Liberty Bar, Jaja, Sylvie in her dressing gown, William buying provisions . . . Or the villa at Antibes, the two Martinis, the old one and the young one, and the old car, in which he took them shopping, . . .

Then look at Harry Brown, who represented the enemy: capable, methodical, virtuous, with his hair so beautifully combed and his dress so correct, his self-possession, his politeness, his secretaries . . .

To annoy them!

Yes, that was William all over. The enemy of order and respectability. A man who could go for days without washing. And to think he'd started life just like his son!

He had become the enemy and was disowned by his family. But he went on fighting! He must have known he could never get the better of them. There was, however, one thing he could do:

Annoy them!

He could annoy his wife and her precious brother and his three sons, who no longer looked upon him as a father but who went on working to make money, always, more money. . . .

"If he died intestate," Brown explained calmly, "the lawsuit would die a natural death, and with it all the scandal, which some people seem to enjoy. . . ."

"Of course."

"But he had made a will. . . . He could not disinherit his wife and children. But he could dispose of part of his fortune. And who do you think were his heirs? . . . Four women."

Maigret could hardly keep a straight face at the thought of those four women arriving in Australia to fight for their rights.

"And that will," said Harry, "is the document you're holding in your hand."

It was long, and looked authentic enough, with the signature of a notary.

"That's what my father was referring to when he said he had 'taken steps.' "

"Did you know the terms of the will?"

"Until today I knew nothing about it. . . . Soon after I got back to the Provençal from the funeral, a man asked to see me."

"Was his name Joseph?"

"He didn't say. He looked like a waiter. He showed me a copy of the will and said that I could buy the original for twenty thousand francs if I went to a certain hotel in Cannes. . . . People like him don't lie about such things."

A frown made Maigret look severe.

"Do you mean to say you've been conspiring to destroy a will?"

The accusation did not appear to trouble Brown in the slightest.

"I know what I'm doing," he answered calmly. "And I think I know how to deal with women of that kind."

He stood up, and catching sight of Maigret's full glass, said: "You're not drinking?"

"No, thank you."

"Any court of justice would understand . . ."

"That your family must win in the end!"

What possessed Maigret to say a thing like that? Had he completely lost his head?

But Harry Brown showed no sign of annoyance. He moved toward the door through which came the clacking of the type-writer.

"The will has not been destroyed," he said quietly. "It's in your possession. . . . I shall be staying here until . . ."

His secretary rushed in with the telephone.

"It's London."

Brown took the receiver and plunged into conversation in English.

Maigret thought it a suitable moment to go. He stuffed the will into his pocket and made his way to the elevator, where he pushed the button in vain. Finally, as he went down the stairs, he repeated:

"Tactful handling!"

In the lobby, Inspector Boutigues and the manager were drinking port from handsome glasses, the bottle between them.

CHAPTER EIGHT

The Four Heiresses

Boutigues bounced along at Maigret's side, and they hadn't taken twenty steps before he announced:

"I've made a discovery! The manager there, whom I've known for a long time, has to keep an eye on another hotel that belongs to the same company. The Hotel du Cap, at Cap Ferrat."

They were leaving the Provençal behind them. In the night the sea in front of them was nothing but an enormous pool of ink.

To the west were the lights murmuring of Cannes; to the east, like fireflies, those of Nice. Boutigues pointed at them in the dark.

"You know Cap Ferrat? . . . Between Nice and Monte Carlo . . ."

Maigret knew. By now he was familiar with the Côte d'Azur, the forty-mile-long esplanade starting at Cannes and ending at Mentone, with villas, luxury hotels, and here and there a casino. The sea, so famous for its blueness . . . The mountains behind . . . A land fulfilling every promise: orange trees, mimosa, sunshine, palms and parasol pines, tearooms, tennis, golf, and American bars . . .

"And the discovery?"

"Well, Harry Brown has a mistress on the Riviera. At Cap Ferrat. The manager knows her by sight. She's a woman about thirty, either a widow or divorced, very respectable. He has rented a villa for her. . . ."

Was Maigret listening? Peevishly he contemplated the spread of sea and mountains. Boutigues went on:

"He goes to see her about once a month. And it's the greatest joke at the Hotel du Cap, because Brown takes absurd precautions to hide what everybody knows. When he spends the night away, he sneaks back into the hotel by the employees' entrance."

"Amusing," said Maigret, but with so little sign of being amused that Boutigues was quite crestfallen.

"Are you going to have him watched?"

"No . . . Yes . . ."

"Will you go and see the woman at Cap Ferrat?"

Maigret hadn't the faintest idea. He couldn't think of half a dozen things at once, and at the moment he wasn't thinking of Harry Brown but of William. When they reached Place Macé, he perfunctorily shook Boutigues' hand and jumped into a taxi.

"Take the road to Cap d'Antibes. I'll tell you when to stop."

Then, leaning back in his seat, he sighed and repeated once again:

"William Brown was murdered."

The little garden gate, the gravel path, a ring at the bell.
. . . A light was switched on inside, there were steps in the
hall, and then the front door opened a few inches.

"Oh, it's you!" said Gina Martini, relieved to see it was the
superintendent. She opened the door wide and stood aside to
let him pass.

A man's voice could be heard in the living room.

"Come in," said Gina.

The man had a notebook and pencil in his hands. Only
half of the old woman was visible; the other half was in a
closet.

"Monsieur Petitfils . . . We asked him to come and help
us."

Monsieur Petitfils was thin and had a long mournful mustache and tired eyes.

"He's head of the biggest real-estate agency here. We wanted
his advice and . . ."

The same smell of musk. The two women had changed
their mourning clothes and were now in dressing gowns and
slippers.

The house was in greater disarray than ever. Were the lights
working properly? The room seemed dingier than before.
The old woman emerged from the closet and started to
explain.

"From the moment I saw those two women at the funeral,
I haven't had a moment's peace. We called in Monsieur Petitfils. . . . He agrees with me that it would be best to make an
inventory."

"An inventory of what?"

"Of the things that belong to us, and that were William's.
We've been at it since two this afternoon."

There were piles of sheets on the table, incongruous objects
on the floor, heaps of books, additional linen in baskets.

Monsieur Petitfils was taking notes, putting a check opposite each item the Martinis claimed.

What could Maigret do here? It would be useless to look for memories of William Brown in this house that was no longer his. In their sortings and classifyings, the women had obliterated all trace of him.

"As for the stove," said the old woman, "it's always been mine. I had it twenty years ago in my place in Toulouse."

"Can we offer you anything, Superintendent?" asked Gina.

On one of the tables was a dirty glass—the agent's. And as he took his notes, he smoked one of Brown's cigars.

"No, thank you. I only came to say . . ."

What had he come to say?

". . . that I hope, tomorrow, to lay hands on the murderer."

"Already?"

But they were obviously not interested at all, and the mother asked:

"You've seen the son, haven't you? . . . What does he say? . . . What's he going to do? . . . Is he coming here to take possession?"

"I don't know . . . I think not."

"It would be shameful. . . . People as rich as that . . . But they're often the worst when it comes to . . ."

She was suffering. The suspense was torture to her. She looked around at all the old things in an agony of fear at the thought of losing them.

And Maigret had his hand in his pocket. He could draw out a piece of paper, unfold it, show it to the two women . . .

What would it do to them? Would it make them delirious with joy? Would it be too much for the mother and kill her?

Millions and millions of francs! Admittedly, they would have to do much more than ask for the money. They would have to go to Australia and fight for it.

And go they would; fight they would. He could just see them! Sailing off with all their dignified airs!

It wouldn't be Monsieur Petitfils whose advice they would be asking, but notaries, lawyers. . . .

"I won't interrupt you any longer. I'll come again tomorrow."

His taxi was waiting for him. He got in without giving an address. The driver held the door open and waited.

"Cannes," said Maigret at last.

The same thoughts chased each other through his mind. Tactful handling . . .

That blessed William! Had he been stabbed in the chest, one would suspect he'd done it himself. Just to annoy everybody. But it wasn't so easy to stab yourself in the back.

William was no longer a puzzle to Maigret. On the contrary, Maigret had the impression he'd known him well, had been his friend always. First, William in Australia: a boy well brought up, rather shy, watched over by his wealthy parents; marrying a suitable girl; the father of three boys . . .

That Brown was just like this other Brown, the son. Sometimes his thoughts would wander unaccountably, and he would be prey to an obscure restlessness. But when that happened, he'd say he was out of sorts and take a purgative.

The same William in Europe: the dikes bursting, a flood of pleasures of every description. . . . And he became a familiar figure along the esplanade from Cannes to Mentone. A yacht in Cannes . . . baccarat in Nice . . . and all the rest of it . . . And a great lassitude about going back "down there."

"Next month, perhaps."

And next month the same words would be repeated.

Then they cut off his livelihood. The brother-in-law woke up! All the Browns and the relatives and tenants struck back.

Things looked different then, though his credit lasted a

while. Then they stopped paying his debts. He got an allowance of five thousand francs a month.

No more yacht. A modest villa.

In the matter of women, too, he came down in the world—down to Gina Martini.

But he had farther to fall. The villa at Antibes was still too bourgeois. He had to hit bottom. So he found the Liberty Bar, Jaja, Sylvie . . .

Meanwhile, the lawsuit dragged on back home, his suit against all the rest of the proper Browns . . . just to annoy them!

And he even made a will—to annoy them after his death.

It wasn't Maigret's business to decide who was right and who was wrong. Yet he couldn't help comparing the two parties: the father, William, versus the son, Harry, so proper, so self-controlled, taking care of everything.

Harry disliked chaos. His thoughts had wandered too, but he had tackled the problem methodically. He kept a mistress tucked away in a villa on Cap Ferrat . . . "very respectable . . . a widow or divorced." He always used the employees' entrance when he returned to his hotel in the early morning.

Order versus chaos . . .

Maigret was the judge. He had only to produce the will from his pocket!

He could catch all four women in that net. It was fascinating to think of William Brown's heiresses arriving in Australia. Jaja with her sore feet, swollen ankles, and drooping breasts. Sylvie, who couldn't bear to wear anything at home except a dressing gown loose around her naked body. Madame Martini with her cheeks plastered with makeup. Gina leaving her inimitable trail of musk.

Meanwhile, Maigret was being driven along the famous boulevard. The lights of Cannes could be seen now.

"A case for tactful handling!"

The taxi stopped opposite the Ambassadors, and the driver asked:

"Where do you want to go?"

"Nowhere. This'll do."

Maigret got out and paid. The Casino was ablaze with light. Fancy cars were arriving. It was close to nine.

At the same time, a dozen other casinos between Cannes and Mentone would be ablaze, and luxurious cars would be gliding toward them.

When Maigret reached the alley, he saw at a glance that the Liberty Bar was closed. It would have been pitch-dark inside but for the street lamp, which dimly showed the bar and the slot machine.

He knocked, and was astonished at the way the sound echoed in the alley. A moment later, a door opened behind him, and a man appeared in the entrance of the bar opposite.

"Is it for Jaja?"

"Yes."

"Who wants her?"

"The superintendent."

"In that case, I have a message for you: She'll be back in a few minutes, and she asked if you'd mind waiting inside. . . ."

"That's all right."

Maigret preferred to walk. In the other bar were some customers he didn't like the look of. A window opened somewhere near, and a woman, having heard the voices, called out cautiously:

"Is that you, Jean?"

"No."

And Maigret, pacing in the alley, said to himself:

"First I must find out who killed William."

Ten o'clock. Jaja had not come back. Each time he heard steps, Maigret started, thinking his wait was at an end. Each time he was disappointed.

He walked barely fifty yards of irregular cobblestones between walls barely more than six feet apart: on one side, the lighted window of a bar; on the other, a dark and lifeless bar. These were old houses with bulging walls and windows no longer rectangular.

Maigret went into the lighted bar.

"She didn't say where she was going?"

"No. Won't you have something?"

The customers, who had been told who he was, examined him from head to foot.

"No, thanks."

He walked to the corner of the alley and stood for a moment at the frontier between the two worlds, the respectable world and the disreputable world.

Half past ten . . . Eleven . . . Not far from the corner of the alley was the café called Harry's Bar. It was where Maigret had telephoned that afternoon, dragging Sylvie with him. He entered and went to the telephone booth.

"Give me police headquarters . . . Hello! Superintendent Maigret speaking . . . Those two birds I brought you this afternoon—has anyone been to see them?"

"Yes. A fat woman."

"Who did she see?"

"The woman first. Then the man . . . We didn't know . . . You left no instructions."

"When was this?'

"A good hour and a half ago. She brought cakes and cigarettes."

Maigret hung up irritably. Then he lifted the receiver again. This time he asked for the Provençal.

"Hello! It's the police! . . . Yes, I'm the one you saw this evening. Will you tell me whether Monsieur Harry Brown has received any visitors?"

"A woman came about fifteen minutes ago. . . . Poorly dressed."

"Where was he?"

"He was in the dining room. She was shown up to his room to wait."

"Has she gone?"

"She went a moment ago."

"A common-looking woman? Very fat?"

"That's right."

"Did she take a taxi?"

"No. She left on foot."

Maigret hung up. He sat down in the bar and ordered choucroute and beer.

So Jaja had seen Sylvie and Joseph . . . They had given her some message for Harry Brown. . . . She'd be coming back by bus, so she couldn't be expected for another half hour.

He picked up a paper that was lying on the table. Two lovers had committed suicide at Bandol. The man had a wife in Czechoslovakia.

"Do you want something else to eat?"

"No, thank you. How much is that? . . . No, wait. Give me another glass of beer."

A little later he was once more in the alley, passing and repassing the dark window of the Liberty Bar. He thought of the Casino. The curtain would be going up on another gala night. Opera and ballet. Then supper and dancing. And gambling constantly.

The same thing all along the coast. Forty miles of it! Hundreds of croupiers sizing up the gamblers; hundreds of women sizing up the men; hundreds of waiters and gigolos sizing up the women . . .

And hundreds of businessmen, like Monsieur Petitfils, with their lists of villas for sale or for rent, sizing up the new arrivals to the Riviera.

But here and there, in Cannes, in Nice, in Monte Carlo, a district darker than the rest, with back alleys, strange old houses, people slinking in the shadows, old women and young women, slot machines, a kitchen behind a bar . . .

The dregs . . .

Still Jaja did not come! Ten times Maigret swung around at the sound of steps. He felt uncomfortable each time he passed the bar opposite, where the barman watched him with a sneer.

At that very moment there were thousands, tens of thousands of sheep on the Brown estates, munching the Browns' grass, herded by the Browns' men. . . . Or perhaps the Browns' men were shearing them—for it would be broad daylight down there.

Wagonloads of wool; cargoes of wool; captains, officers, crews. Ships putting out to sea; officers checking the temperature in the holds. Then the brokers in Amsterdam, London, Liverpool, Le Havre, discussing the prices.

And Harry Brown in his suite at the Provençal receiving cables from his brothers, from his uncle; making telephone calls to his agents.

In the newspaper at the bar, Maigret read:

DAUGHTER OF MUSLIM RULER MARRIED TO PRINCE

And it went on to say:

"In honor of the occasion, elaborate festivities have been taking place in India, in Iran, in Afghanistan, in . . ."

And then, farther on:

"A formal dinner was given in Nice in the Palais de la Méditerranée. Prominent among the guests were . . .

A princess marrying in Nice, and champagne flowing all along the forty-mile coast . . . While back in the Middle East, the devil knows where, hundred of thousands of people were . . .

Still no Jaja! Maigret knew every cobblestone by this time and every detail of the houses along the alley. A young girl with braids was sitting at one of the windows struggling to finish her homework.

Had the bus met with an accident? Had Jaja gone on somewhere else? Had she run away? Peering in through the window of the Liberty Bar, he could see the cat licking its paws.

Scraps from the newspaper kept coming back to him.

"Traveling incognito, the King arrived yesterday and proceeded to his Cap Ferrat estate, accompanied by . . ."

And:

"Early this morning Monsieur Graphopoulos was arrested in Nice, shortly after winning five thousand francs in a *salle de baccarat*. He is accused of cheating."

Then this short paragraph:

"The deputy director of the police in charge of gambling may be involved."

Of course! If a William Brown yielded to temptation, how could one expect a poor devil earning two thousand francs a month to be a hero?

Maigret was fed up. Fed up with waiting. Fed up with an investigation that was not in his line at all.

Why had they sent him here with such absurd instructions? Tactful handling. No awkward revelations.

And suppose he wasn't tactful? Suppose he produced the will? Suppose the four women did go to Australia? . . .

Steps . . . This time he didn't bother to look around, until a key turned in a lock and a tired voice said:

"So you're here."

It was Jaja. An exhausted Jaja. Her hand trembled as she removed the key. Jaja in all her finery; mauve coat and blood-red shoes.

"Come in . . . Just a minute . . . I'll switch on the light."

The cat promptly began purring and rubbing against her swollen legs. She groped for the switch.

"When I think of that poor Sylvie . . ."

At last she switched on the light, and they could see their way. The barman opposite had his nasty face right against the window.

"Do come in . . . My legs will hardly hold me up. . . . And what with my feelings . . ."

She went straight to the stove, where the fire was glowing, stirred it up, and shifted a saucepan.

"Sit down, Superintendent. I'll get changed, but I'll be down again in a moment."

She had not once looked at Maigret. With her back to him, she repeated:

"That poor Sylvie . . ."

She went upstairs and began taking off her things, talking all the time.

"A good girl . . . If she had wanted . . . It's always those who pay for the others. . . . Again and again I've told her . . ."

Maigret sat down at the table, on which were the remains of some cheese and sardines. He could hear every movement Jaja made as she waddled to and fro in the room above, particularly the jig she danced, trying not to lose her balance as she took off her shoes.

CHAPTER NINE

Haguenau

"With all I've been through . . . and my feet, they're so swollen . . ."

Jaja had stopped moving around in the bedroom. Sitting in a chair, she was woefully rubbing her bare feet as she spoke.

She raised her voice so that Maigret could hear in the room below; and she was astonished, on looking up, to see him standing at the top of the stairs.

"Oh! I didn't know you were there. . . . I'm afraid the place is an awful mess—but don't take any notice of that. Since all this trouble began . . ."

Maigret would have found it hard to say why he went up. Listening to her chatter, it had occurred to him that he had never seen the upstairs room.

Now he stood looking around while Jaja continued to massage her feet and talked on, becoming more and more voluble.

"Have I eaten? . . . I don't think I have. . . . It gave me a turn to see Sylvie there."

She had slipped her dressing gown loosely over her bright pink underclothes, which were fringed with lace and contrasted with her inordinately white skin. The bed was still unmade, and Maigret could not help thinking that nobody seeing him there would have believed he had come only to talk.

The room was quite ordinary, apart from its untidiness, and better furnished than one might have expected. The mahogany bed looked thoroughly bourgeois. A round table. A wardrobe. A chest of drawers. On the other hand, the slop pail was in the middle of the room, and the table was littered with powders, face creams, and dirty towels.

Jaja sighed as she finally put on her slippers.

"I wonder how it'll end."

"It's here that William used to sleep when . . . ?"

"There's only this room and the two downstairs."

In a corner was a couch upholstered in shabby velveteen.

"He slept on that couch?"

"Sometimes . . . Sometimes I did."

"And Sylvie?"

"With me."

The room was so low that Maigret's hat touched the ceiling. On the narrow window were green curtains. The electric light had no shade.

It took a great effort of the imagination to picture life in that room. William and Jaja, drunk, tottering up to bed. Then Sylvie coming in and slipping into bed beside Fat Jaja.

But in the morning? In daylight?

Jaja had never chattered so much. She spoke plaintively, as though wanting pity.

"I'm so upset, I'm sure to be sick. I always am. . . . It happened when some sailors had a fight just outside the bar

108

. . . three years ago now . . . and one of them got slashed with a razor. . . ."

She stood up and began to look for something, then forgot what it was.

"And what about you? Have you had anything to eat? . . . Come down, and I'll see what I can find."

Maigret led the way down. Jaja went to the stove, put more coal in, and stirred something in the saucepan.

"I haven't the heart to cook when I'm alone. . . . And when I think of where Sylvie is . . ."

"Tell me, Jaja . . ."

"What?"

"What was it Sylvie said to you, this afternoon, while I was serving that man in the bar?"

"Yes . . . I asked her about the twenty thousand francs. She said she didn't know; that it was some scheme of Joseph's."

"And this evening?"

"What do you mean?"

"When you saw her at the police station?"

"The same. She didn't know, and she was wondering what Joseph had been up to."

"Has she been with Joseph a long time?"

"She's with him, and at the same time she's not. . . . They don't live together. . . . She met him somewhere—at the races, I suppose—anyhow, it wasn't here. He said he could do her a good turn, introduce her to clients. . . . Of course, he could, being a waiter! He's been well brought up. Educated, too. Though that doesn't change the fact that I never liked him."

From a saucepan, Jaja poured lentils onto a plate.

"Wouldn't you like some? . . . No? . . . Well, help yourself to something to drink. . . . I don't feel up to cooking. . . . Is the door of the bar shut?"

Maigret was sitting astride his chair, as he had that afternoon. He watched her eat, listened while she talked.

"You see, those people—and the casino waiters most of all—are clever, and think of things we could never understand. . . . And if anything goes wrong, it's sure to be the woman who gets arrested. . . . Now if Sylvie had listened to me . . ."

"And what was the errand Joseph sent you on this evening?"

She stared at Maigret with her mouth full, as though unable to understand. But after a moment she went on:

"Oh, yes! . . . To the son . . ."

"What was it you were to say to him?"

"That he was to get Sylvie released; otherwise . . ."

"Otherwise what?"

"Oh, I know you won't give me a moment's peace. Though you must admit I've treated you fair and square. . . . I'm doing my best, aren't I? I have nothing to hide."

He guessed why she was so talkative, and her voice so tearful. She had stopped in more than one bistro on the way home to give herself courage.

"At first, it was me who was always holding Sylvie back, stopping her from joining Joseph for good. . . . And then, when I understood he'd been up to something . . ."

"Well?"

It was really more comical than pathetic. Still eating, she began to cry. It was a preposterous sight: a fat woman in a purple dressing gown sitting over a plate of lentils and whimpering like a child.

"Don't bully me. Give me time to think. . . . With all this trouble, my head's spinning. . . . Give me something to drink."

"In a minute."

"Let me have something to drink, and I'll tell you everything."

He poured her a small glass of whiskey.

"Now, what is it you want to know? . . . What was I saying? . . . Oh, yes! When I saw the twenty thousand francs . . . Were they in William's pocket?"

It cost Maigret an effort to keep his head from spinning, too, as he listened to Jaja's tortuous ramblings. But at the same time a gleam of comprehension was dawning in his mind.

"From William's pocket? . . ." Jaja must have assumed the money was taken from Brown when he was killed. "Was that what you thought?"

"I don't know what I thought. . . . There! I can't eat another mouthful. . . . Do you have a cigarette?"

"I only smoke a pipe."

"There ought to be a cigarette somewhere. Sylvie always has some."

She poked around in drawers, but couldn't find any.

"Do they always send them to Alsace?"

"Who? . . . What? . . . What are you talking about?"

"Women . . . What's the place called? That prison . . . I know it begins with Hau. . . . In my time . . ."

"When you were in Paris?"

"Yes. They were always talking about it. . . . They used to say it was so strict that lots of women tried to kill themselves. . . . And not so long ago I read in the paper that there are convicts there who are eighty years old. . . . No, there are no cigarettes. Sylvie must have taken them with her."

"And she's afraid of going there?"

"Sylvie? . . . I don't know. . . . I was thinking about it on the bus. There was an old woman in front of me, and . . ."

"Sit down."

"Yes . . . Pay no attention to me . . . I'm not myself. . . . What were we talking about?"

A look of anxiety came into her eyes. She ran her hand across her forehead, causing a wisp of hair with a tinge of red to fall on her cheek.

"It makes me sad. . . . Pour me another drink, will you?"

"When you've told me what you know."

"But I don't know anything! What should I know? . . . First, I saw Sylvie. . . . And even so, there was a cop standing over us the whole time, listening to what we said. . . . And I did so want to cry. . . . When Sylvie kissed me good-bye, she whispered in my ear that it was all Joseph's fault."

"Then you saw him?"

"Yes. I told you that before. . . . He sent me to Juan-les-Pins to warn Brown that if . . ."

She was groping for words. Sometimes her mind seemed to slip, as it does with some drunkards. At such moments she would look at Maigret as though she were drowning and longed to catch hold of him.

"I don't know any more. . . . I can't stand it. . . . I'm just a poor woman who's always tried to have a kind word for everybody."

"No! Not yet!"

Maigret snatched the bottle she had picked up. He could see what would happen: all of a sudden she'd be dead drunk and asleep.

"You saw Harry Brown?"

"No . . . Yes . . . He said if I crossed his path again he'd have me locked up, too."

Then, suddenly jubilant:

"Hossegor! . . . No, that's not right either. Hossegor's something else. . . . It's in a story. . . . Haguenau! That's the place!"

The name of the prison.

"They say they're not even allowed to speak. . . . Do you think that's true?"

Never had she been, in Maigret's presence, so incoherent. It was enough to make one wonder whether her mind was going.

"Of course," he said, "if Sylvie's an accomplice, she'll be sent to—"

Jaja interrupted him hurriedly, talking faster than ever, feverishly, while blood mounted to her face.

"Tonight, I've finally understood a thing or two. Those twenty thousand francs, for instance—I know now what they were for. It's William's son—that fellow Harry—who gave them to her, to pay for . . ."

"To pay for what?"

"Everything!" said Jaja triumphantly, giving him a look of defiance. "You see, I'm not such a fool. . . . And when the son heard there was a will . . ."

"Excuse me. You know about it?"

"It was last month that William spoke of it. . . . We were here, all four of us. . . ."

"You and he, Sylvie and Joseph?"

"Yes. . . . We'd been drinking a lot, because it was William's birthday. . . . And we got to talking about all kinds of things. When he drank, he talked about Australia, about his wife, his brother-in-law. . . ."

"What did he say?"

"That they'd all be surprised at his death. And he whipped the will out of his pocket and started reading it aloud. . . . He didn't read it all, not the part about the other two women. . . . He said he'd been to a lawyer."

"A month ago? . . . At that time, did Joseph know of Harry Brown?"

"You can never tell with him. Being a waiter, he picks up things."

"And do you think he might have told the son?"

"I didn't say that! I didn't say anything of the kind. Only, you can't help thinking, can you? . . . You know, those rich people are no better than us. . . . Well, suppose Joseph had gone and told him . . . And suppose young Brown had said, in a casual sort of way, that he'd like to have that will. . . . But what use would the will be to him as long as William was alive? Couldn't William easily make another?"

Maigret was off guard, and she had poured herself a glass and swallowed it before he could stop her. She leaned over toward him, her alcoholic breath right in his face. Lowering her voice dramatically, she continued:

"And once he was dead . . . You see what I'm saying? . . . Then there'd be the price to discuss . . . For twenty thousand francs . . . Or maybe double . . . He might have paid Joseph twenty thousand in advance. You never know. . . . I'm only saying what comes into my head, of course. But things like that aren't usually paid for all at once. . . . As for Sylvie . . ."

"She wouldn't know anything about it?"

"If she'd known, I'd have known. . . . Was that someone knocking?"

She sat petrified with fear. To reassure her, Maigret had to go to the street door. When he returned, he found she had taken the opportunity to have another drink.

"Don't think I've told you anything. I haven't. I don't know anything. . . . You see what I mean? . . . I'm only a poor woman who's lost her husband, who . . ."

Once more she burst into tears. This time, it wasn't comical. It was painful.

"According to you, Jaja, what would William have been

doing that Friday afternoon between two o'clock and five?"

She looked at him without answering, still crying. But her sobs now were unconvincing.

"Sylvie had left just ahead of him," Maigret went on. "Don't you think they might have . . . ?"

"Who?"

"Sylvie and William?"

"That they might have what?"

"How should I know? . . . Met somewhere, perhaps? . . . After all, Sylvie's young and attractive. . . . And William . . ."

He watched Jaja closely. Pretending indifference, he continued:

"They might have met somewhere. Joseph would be in hiding. And at the right moment he'd spring out and stab William in the back."

Jaja said nothing. She gaped at him, frowned, as though making a tremendous effort to follow what he was saying. In her condition, this was not easy. Her eyes were unfocused, and her thoughts were no doubt wandering.

"Harry Brown, hearing of the will, suggests the crime. Sylvie decoys William to the spot. Joseph does the deed. . . . Then Harry Brown is told to bring the money to Sylvie, in a hotel in Cannes."

Jaja didn't move. Was she too taken aback to speak? Or didn't she understand a word?

"Joseph, arrested, sends you to tell Harry he'll spill the beans if he's not set free."

Jaja shouted:

"That's it! Yes, that's it!"

She stood up. She panted. As if torn between a desire to cry and a need to burst out laughing.

Suddenly she put both hands to her head convulsively. Her hair fell loose. She stamped with impatience.

"Yes, that's it! And me thinking . . . I don't know . . . I . . . I . . ."

Maigret sat still, looking at her with astonishment. Was she becoming hysterical?

"I . . . I . . ."

This was unexpected. She seized the bottle and threw it on the floor, where it smashed into pieces.

"And me thinking . . ."

The light in the alley outside was faint through the two doors. The barman opposite could be heard putting up his shutters. It must have been very late. The streetcars had stopped ages ago.

"I can't bear the thought of it," she shrieked. "I can't. . . . I won't. . . . Anything but *that* . . . It's not true. . . . It's . . ."

"Jaja!"

But the sound of her name did not calm her. She had worked herself into a frenzy. With the same impetuosity with which she had seized the bottle, she stooped and picked up something from the floor.

"Not Haguenau! . . . It's not true. Sylvie didn't . . ."

In all his years of service, Maigret had seen nothing like this. She had picked up a small piece of glass and, talking all the time, had cut into her wrist, right down to the artery.

Her eyes almost popped out of her head. She looked raving mad.

"Haguenau . . . I . . . It wasn't Sylvie!"

A gush of blood spurted out as Maigret reached her. His right hand was covered with it, and it even splashed on his tie. He seized her by both arms.

For a few seconds Jaja, bewildered, helpless, looked at the blood—her own blood—as it ran down. She fainted. Maigret let her sink to the floor.

His fingers felt for the artery and pressed it. But that was no good—he must find something to tie it with. He looked around the room. Spotting an electric cord, he wrenched it free of the iron it belonged to.

As Jaja lay motionless on the floor, he wound the cord around her wrist, and tightened it.

Out in the alley, he hesitated. The bar opposite was closed. In the cool night air, he strode to the street at the end.

There were no lights anywhere except for the streetlights and the Casino. He could see the parked cars, chauffeurs standing in groups by the harbor, and the masts of the yachts, pointing straight and motionless, to the sky.

Not far off, at the cross street, a policeman was on duty.

"Get a doctor! Quick! To the Liberty Bar!"

"Is that the little place down the alley, where . . . ?"

"Yes. The little place where!" snapped Maigret. "And for the love of God, hurry!"

CHAPTER TEN

The Couch

The two policemen did their best to be gentle as they carried the body up the narrow stairs. But Jaja was heavy. Sometimes she was bumped against the wall, sometimes against the banisters, and once or twice she was almost bent double, and her rear end dragged from one step to another.

The doctor, waiting to go up, looked around with curiosity. A whimpering moan filled the rooms, both upstairs and down. It seemed to come from nowhere, though in fact it came from Jaja.

In the low bedroom, Maigret pulled back the sheets and helped the two policemen hoist Jaja onto the bed. She was limp, a dead weight, though she looked like a large stuffed doll.

Did she know what was going on? Did she know where she was? From time to time her eyes opened, but they focused on nothing.

The moan she uttered came out softly, regularly, without the urgency of pain.

"Is she suffering much?" asked Maigret of the doctor, a little old man, kind and punctilious, who was astonished to find himself in such surroundings.

"She should be in no pain. Perhaps she's frightened."

"Is she conscious?"

"She doesn't appear to be. Although . . ."

"She's dead drunk," said Maigret with a sigh. "I thought the pain might have sobered her up."

The two policemen, waiting for further instructions, also looked around the room with curiosity. The curtains were not closed, and behind a window opposite, Maigret could see a pale face in an unlighted room. He drew the curtains, then beckoned to one of the policemen.

"Go get the girl I had locked up. Sylvie, she's called. . . . But not the man."

And, turning to the other:

"Wait for me downstairs."

The doctor did what was necessary to the severed artery, then stood by the bed looking at the fat woman, who still moaned. He seemed at a loss. To cover his indecision, he took her pulse, felt her hands, her forehead.

"A word with you, doctor," said Maigret from the corner of the room.

When the doctor came over to him, he continued in an undertone:

"I'd like you to take the opportunity to examine her. If you could give me a rough idea . . ."

"Certainly."

The little doctor seemed more and more perplexed. He was probably wondering whether Maigret was a relative of the patient. He opened his bag. Methodically, he set about taking her blood pressure.

Dissatisfied, he took it three times. Then he opened her dressing gown to listen to her heart. Like most French doctors, he did not use a stethoscope, and he looked around for a clean cloth to put between his ear and her chest. There being none in the room, he had to use his handkerchief.

When he was finished, he muttered:

"Yes."

"Yes what?"

"She'll never know old age! The heart's enlarged and almost worn out. As for her blood pressure, it's dreadful."

"How long do you give her?"

"That's another question. . . . If she were one of my patients, I'd send her to the country. Complete rest, absolute quiet, a strict diet . . ."

"No alcohol, of course."

"That's the most important thing of all."

"And that would save her?"

"I wouldn't say that. But it would keep her going for a year or two."

They stopped, suddenly conscious of the silence around them. Something was missing. It was Jaja's moaning.

When they turned to the bed, they found her raised on an elbow, a fierce look in her eyes, her chest heaving.

She had heard. She had understood. And glared at the little doctor, as though holding him responsible for her condition. Feebly, the doctor asked:

"Do you feel better?"

Her lips curled contemptuously. Without a word, she lay down and closed her eyes.

The doctor, doubting that he was wanted any longer, started

putting away his instruments. As he did so, he apparently talked to himself, for every now and then he nodded approvingly.

"I suppose that's all," said Maigret finally. "There's nothing to fear, then?"

"Not for the moment, anyhow."

As soon as the doctor left, Maigret placed a chair by the foot of the bed, sat down, and lighted his pipe, to mask the disgusting antiseptic smell. Nor did he like the look of the basin of water that had been used to wash the wound. He pushed it out of sight under the wardrobe.

Quietly, pensively, he sat and regarded Jaja's face, which seemed all curves. Round cheeks and, now that her hair was thrown back, a large rounded forehead with a little scar on one of the temples.

To the left of the bed was the couch.

Jaja wasn't sleeping. Of that he was sure. Her breathing was irregular, and her eyelids quivered.

What was she thinking about? She knew he was there and looking at her. And she knew now that her engine was running down, and that she had not much longer to live.

What images fluttered behind that rounded forehead?

Suddenly frantic again, she sat up with a jerk, looked at Maigret with wild eyes, and cried out:

"Don't leave me! . . . I'm afraid! . . . Where's he gone? Where's that little man? . . . I don't want to . . ."

Maigret stood up and bent over her. He couldn't keep a tender note from coming into his voice as he said:

"It's all right, old thing. Just be quiet."

That's what she was—an old thing. A poor old thing soaked in alcohol, with legs so swollen that she walked like an elephant.

Yet in her day she had promenaded up and down miles of sidewalk near Porte Saint-Martin.

She let him push her head gently back on the pillow. She was sober now. The policeman downstairs had found a bottle and was pouring himself a drink. Jaja heard and asked anxiously:

"Who's that?"

And other sounds reached them—steps in the alley and the voice of a woman, breathless from walking so fast, asking:

"Why is the bar dark? What's the . . . ?"

"Quiet! Don't make any noise."

In answer to a light knock on the shutter, the policeman downstairs opened the door. There were steps across the bar, across the kitchen, then up the stairs.

Jaja, panicky, looked at Maigret. She almost cried out as he went to the door and opened it.

"You can go, you two," he said, standing aside to let Sylvie pass.

Sylvie stopped abruptly in the middle of the room, her hand on her thumping heart. She had forgotten her hat. Not understanding, she stared fixedly at the bed.

"Jaja . . ."

Downstairs, the one who had had a drink was pouring again. There was a clink as glasses touched. Then the door of the bar opened and shut; steps gradually receded toward the harbor.

Maigret was so still and silent that his presence was hardly noticeable.

"My poor Jaja . . ."

Yet Sylvie went no nearer. Something held her back: the stony stare with which the older woman greeted her.

Turning to Maigret, Sylvie stammered:

"Is it . . . ?"

"Is it what?"

"Nothing . . . I don't know. . . . What's the matter?"

Then, a strange thing: in spite of the distance and the closed door, the ticking of the clock below was distinctly audible, so fast, so jerky, that it was as though the clock, in its haste, would dash itself to pieces.

Jaja was nearing another crisis. You could feel it coming, stirring her limp body, kindling her eyes, parching her throat. But she tried as hard as she could to hold it back. Meanwhile, Sylvie remained standing in the middle of the room, confused, with her head lowered and her hands clasped across her chest. She didn't know what to say or do.

Maigret smoked calmly, letting things take their course. He knew that he had closed the circle.

There was no longer any mystery. No unforeseen element could crop up now. All the characters had fallen into place: the two Martinis, the young one and the old, who were perhaps still making their inventory with the help of Monsieur Petitfils; Harry Brown at the Provençal, waiting unperturbed for the conclusion of the investigation, and in the meantime running his business by cable and telephone; Joseph under lock and key . . .

At last Jaja could contain herself no longer. With a look of rage, she pointed at Sylvie with her unwounded hand.

"It's her! . . . The snake! . . . Filthy little . . ."

She brought out the worst word in her vocabulary. Tears ran down from under her eyelids.

"I hate her! Do you hear? I hate her. . . . She fooled me for a long time. . . . And behind my back she called me the old woman. Yes, the old woman! . . . And hadn't I . . ."

"Lie down, Jaja," said Maigret. "You'll make yourself sick."

"Oh, you . . ."

And with renewed fury she went on:

"But I won't let her get away with it. . . . I won't go to

Haguenau. Do you understand? . . . Or if I do, she'll have to go, too."

Her throat was so dry that she looked around instinctively for something to drink.

"Go get a bottle," said Maigret to Sylvie.

"But . . . she's already . . ."

"Go!"

He walked over to the window to make sure the curtains were drawn so that nobody could see them from the window opposite.

"Of course you'll stand up for her, because she's young. . . . I wouldn't be surprised if she's already tried it with you."

Sylvie returned. There were shadows under her eyes. She handed Maigret a half-full bottle of rum.

Jaja sneered.

"Now that I'm finished, you don't care how much I drink! I heard the doctor. . . ."

And the thought of it made her more agitated. She was afraid of dying. Her eyes grew wild.

Even so, she took the bottle and gulped greedily, looking from one to the other of her two companions.

"The old woman who's going to die! . . . But I won't! I won't die before she does. . . . Because it's all her fault."

She broke off like someone who has lost the thread. Maigret sat still, waiting.

"She's talked? I know she's talked, or they wouldn't have let her out. . . . And wasn't I all the time doing my best for her? . . . And it's not true that Joseph sent me to the son. I went on my own. . . . Do you understand?"

Of course! Maigret understood. He had understood for the last hour or more.

He pointed to the couch.

"It wasn't William who slept there, was it?"

"No, it wasn't. He slept here in this bed. In *my* bed . . . William was *my* lover! William came for *me*, for me only! And that creature, who received my charity, she slept on the couch."

She shouted this hoarsely. She only had to be left alone now, and it would all come out. It had to. It was welling up from her innermost being—all that she had been hiding and suppressing. This was the real Jaja, Jaja stripped of her last shreds of reserve.

"The truth is that I loved him, and he loved me. . . . He understood. He knew that if I'd never been educated or taught fine manners, it wasn't my fault. . . . He was happy here with me. Many's the time he told me so. . . . It hurt him to leave me, and when he came back, he was like a schoolboy home on vacation."

She wept as she spoke. Her face was pitiful in the harsh light of the unshaded lamp.

And with one arm bandaged . . .

"I never suspected a thing. I was a fool. But one always is a fool in such cases. . . . She had nowhere to go, and I took her in out of the kindness of my heart. And I kept her here, thinking it would brighten the place up, to have some youth around."

Sylvie did not move.

"Look at her! Stands there as meek as a lamb, but she's sneering at me all the time. She's always been the same, but, idiot that I was, I thought she was shy and frightened. It went straight to my heart. . . . And to think it was in my dressing gowns that she got him, by showing all she had to show!

"She wanted him. She and that pimp of hers, Joseph. It didn't take him long to guess that William had money somewhere. . . .

"Then there was the will. . . ."

She snatched the bottle and drank so greedily that it gurgled in her throat. Sylvie took the opportunity to cast an imploring glance at Maigret. She swayed slightly, hardly able to stand.

"It was from this room that Joseph stole it. . . . I don't know when. No doubt some night we'd had a drop too much. William had talked about it. . . . And Joseph knew that with that paper he could get the son to pay. . . ."

Maigret listened without emotion. Once again he looked around the room. The bed, the couch . . .

William and Jaja . . .

And Sylvie on the couch . . .

Poor William—he couldn't help comparing them.

"No. I never suspected a thing till I saw Sylvie give him a look as she went out after lunch. . . . Even then, I couldn't believe . . . But she'd hardly been gone a minute when he said he'd be going, too. . . . Usually, he never left until the evening. . . . I didn't say anything, . . . I went and put my things on."

She was coming to the critical part, which Maigret had figured out some time ago. He could see it all:

Joseph making a short visit, and leaving with the will now in his pocket. Sylvie dressing before lunch, to be ready to go out right after. A significant look in William's direction as she goes.

And Jaja sees it.

She says nothing, goes on eating and drinking. But no sooner has William gone than she slips her coat on over her housedress.

Nobody left in the bar. An empty house, the door locked. . . .

They ran one after the other. . . .

"Do you know where she met him? . . . At the Hotel Beauséjour. And I was left standing in the street, not knowing what to do with myself. . . . I wanted to go in and knock on their door, to beg Sylvie to give him back to me. . . . There was a cutler's at the corner. . . . And while they were . . . while they were up there, I stared at the shop window. . . . I hardly knew what I was doing. I ached in every limb. . . .

"I went in. . . . I bought a knife without thinking. . . .

"Then they came out, those two. William was glowing; he looked younger. . . . I watched him take her into a shop to buy her a box of chocolates. . . .

"They went off toward the garage. . . . I went as fast as I could, to get outside town before he passed. I knew he'd be coming along the road to Antibes. . . .

"As soon as he saw me, he stopped the car and opened the door. . . .

"And I said to him: 'I've got something for you! Here! And it's for her too!' "

Jaja fell back on her pillow, her shoulders heaving, her face bathed in tears and sweat.

"I don't know what happened next. I suppose he pushed me out and closed the door. . . . I didn't have the knife. I must have dropped it in the car."

That was the only detail Maigret had not thought of. William, his eyes already growing dim, must have had the presence of mind to throw the knife into some bushes.

"It was late when I got back."

Of course. She must have stopped at many a bar.

"I woke up in my bed, very sick. . . ."

She sat up once more.

"But I won't go to Haguenau! I won't! . . . You can do your worst. The doctor said I'm going to die. . . . And this little slut . . ."

A chair scraped on the floor. Sylvie had dragged it over just in time to sink into it sideways. ·She fainted slowly, but it wasn't faked. Her nostrils were pinched, and there was a yellowish tinge about them.

"Serves her right!" cried Jaja. "Let her alone . . . At least . . . I don't know. . . . I don't know anything. . . . Perhaps it's all Joseph's fault . . . Sylvie! My littleSylvie! . . ."

Maigret bent over the girl and slapped her hands and her cheeks. He saw Jaja seize the bottle and drink again, literally pouring the rum down her throat, after which she broke into a desperate fit of coughing.

At last she sighed and buried her face in her pillow.

Maigret picked Sylvie up and carried her downstairs, where he splashed her face with cold water.

The first thing she said when she opened her eyes was:

"It isn't true."

The voice of despair.

"It isn't true. . . . You *must* understand. . . . I don't want to make myself out better than I am. But I'm not as bad as that. I love Jaja! . . . It was he who . . . Do you understand? . . . He began looking at me differently. And for months he kept on begging me. . . . How could I refuse him, when every night . . . with other men . . . ?"

"Shh! Speak quietly."

"Let her hear. If she thinks about it, she'll understand. . . . And when I did give in, I didn't even want Joseph to know. I was afraid he'd take advantage of it. . . . We arranged to meet at . . ."

"Was that the only time?"

"The only time. So you see . . . It's true about the chocolates. . . . He was wild, so wild that I was afraid. . . . He treated me as if . . . as if I weren't a . . ."

"That's all?"

"I had no idea it was Jaja, who . . . I swear! I thought it might be Joseph. . . . I was afraid. . . . He told me to return to the Beauséjour, where somebody was to bring memoney."

And, in a lower voice:

"What else could I have done?"

The moaning started again upstairs—the same high-pitched moaning as before.

"Is she badly hurt?"

Maigret shrugged and went upstairs. Jaja was in a deep sleep. He went down again, and told Sylvie:

"Hush. She's asleep."

There was a note in Maigret's voice that puzzled her. She watched him as he filled another pipe.

"Stay with her. And when she wakes, tell her that I've gone—for good."

"But . . ."

"Tell her she's been dreaming, that she's had a nightmare . . ."

"But . . . I don't understand. . . . and Joseph?"

Standing with his hands in his pockets, he looked into her eyes. Then from one of the pockets he drew out the twenty thousand francs and put them on the table.

"You love him?"

"One has to have a man. Otherwise . . ."

"And William?"

"William was different. He wasn't one of us. He was . . ."

Maigret walked to the door. As he turned the knob, he looked back.

"The Liberty Bar had better be forgotten. Understand?"

As the outer door opened, the early-morning air could be felt. A damp chill was rising from the ground, almost like a mist.

"I never thought you were like that," stammered Sylvie. "I . . . Jaja . . . I tell you she's the best woman in the world."

He turned again, nodded, then walked down to the harbor, where he stopped to relight his pipe.

CHAPTER ELEVEN

A *Love Story*

Maigret uncrossed his legs and, leaning forward, offered the document.

"I can . . . ?" asked Harry Brown, glancing at the door, behind which were his secretary and his typist.

"It's yours."

"Note that I'm ready to treat them liberally. I was thinking of a hundred thousand francs to each of them. I hope you understand. It's not the money I'm concerned about. It's the scandal. . . . If those four women showed up down there . . ."

"I understand."

Through the window could be seen the beach of Juan-les-Pins: a hundred people in bathing suits lying on the sand; three girls doing physical exercises under the eye of a tall, thin instructor; an Algerian going from group to group with a basket of peanuts.

"What do you think of a hundred thousand each?"

"Excellent!" said Maigret, rising.

"You haven't touched your glass."

"No, thanks."

The well-dressed, well-groomed Harry Brown hesitated.

"Do you know, Superintendent," he ventured at last, "for a while I thought you were an adversary. In France. . . ."

"Yes?" said Maigret, moving toward the door.

Brown followed him. There was less assurance in his voice as he went on:

"In France, scandal doesn't matter so much as in . . ."

"Good day, monsieur."

Maigret bowed without offering his hand, and left the temporary headquarters of the wool business.

"In France! . . . In France! . . ." he muttered as he walked down the carpeted stairs.

What about France? What did Frenchmen call Harry Brown's relationship with that quiet, respectable woman at Cap Ferrat? An affair!

And didn't the same expression fit William's liaison with Jaja, with Sylvie?

Walking along the beach, Maigret had to thread his way between half-naked bodies. All around him were bronzed skins, set off by brightly colored bathing suits.

Boutigues was waiting for him by the physical-culture instructor's hut.

"Well?"

"It's all over. . . . William Brown was killed by a person or persons unknown, who robbed him of his wallet."

"But still . . ."

"But what? . . . Don't muddy the water!" Maigret repeated,

staring at the blue water, which was calm as a millpond, and the little boats. . . . This was certainly not the place to make trouble.

"You see that girl in the green bathing suit?"

"The one with the skinny thighs?"

"You'll never guess who she is," said Boutigues triumphantly. "Morrow's daughter."

"Morrow?"

"The diamond man. One of the dozen richest men in . . ."

The sun was hot. Maigret, in his black suit and bowler, made the one dark spot on the landscape. The sound of music drifted down from a casino.

"Shall we have a drink?"

Boutigues, of course, was wearing his light gray suit and had a carnation in his buttonhole.

"As I said before, on the Riviera we . . ."

"On the Riviera . . ."

"You don't like it on the Riviera?"

With a lyrical sweep of his arm, he pointed to the bay, so wonderful a blue, to Cap d'Antibes with its white villas half hidden in the greenery, to the Casino, yellow as custard, and to the palms along the promenade . . .

"That stout man over there in the striped bathing suit—he's editor of one of the biggest papers in Germany."

After a sleepless night, Maigret's eyes were gray. All he could do was grunt:

"And what if he is?"

"I've made you some creamed salt cod. Is that all right?"

"As if you need to ask."

Boulevard Richard-Lenoir; Maigret's apartment, through whose windows a few scraggly chestnut trees were visible.

"What was it all about?" asked Madame Maigret.

"An affair. But since they'd told me to be tactful . . ."

With both elbows on the table, he was thoroughly enjoying the cod. He spoke with his mouth full.

"An Australian who'd had enough of Australia and its sheep."

"What do you mean?"

"An Australian who kicked over the traces, and did it pretty thoroughly."

"And then?"

"Then . . . Nothing much. He had a glorious binge until his wife and his brother-in-law and his children cut off his means."

"That's not very interesting."

"Not in the least. That's what I'm saying. . . . He went on living on the Riviera . . ."

"It must be beautiful down there."

"Magnificent! . . . He rented a villa. Then, in order not to be too lonely, he had someone come live with him."

"A woman! I begin to understand."

"I wonder? . . . Pass the sauce, will you? . . . You might have put a little more onion in it."

"It's these onions you get in Paris. They have no flavor at all. I used a whole pound. . . . But go on."

"So the woman came, but she brought along her mother."

"Her mother?"

"Yes . . . But it rather spoiled the charm. So he began to look for amusement elsewhere."

"He took a mistress?"

"He already had one! And her mother. What he found was a low-class bar with a nice, fat, kind woman to drink with him."

"She drank?"

134

"Yes. They both did. And after a while they'd talk a lot, about everything."

"And then?"

"The old woman thought it had come."

"What had come?"

"Love! That somebody loved her, that she'd found a kindred spirit, and all the rest of it."

"All the rest of what?"

"Nothing . . . They made a good couple. Both getting on. And they could keep up with each other—glass for glass."

"What happened?"

"She'd taken a little protégée, a girl named Sylvie. And in the end the Australian fell for Sylvie."

Madame Maigret looked reproachfully at her husband.

"It's not a very pretty story you're telling me."

"It's the truth. He fell for her, but Sylvie wasn't having it, because of the old woman. Then she finally gave in, because, after all, the Australian was the principal character."

"I don't follow that."

"It doesn't matter. . . . The Australian and the little one met in a hotel."

"Behind the old woman's back?"

"Exactly. You follow me perfectly. But the old one found out. And when she realized she was being left out in the cold, she killed her lover. . . . Really, this cod is a triumph."

"I still don't understand."

"What don't you understand?"

"Why you didn't arrest the old woman. After all, she . . ."

"Not at all."

"What do you mean?"

"Give me some more, first . . . Thanks . . . That's not what I was sent for. I wasn't sent to make trouble. To muddy the

water. And the wife and the brother-in-law and the sons in
Australia are very important people, and rich enough to pay
a lot of money for a will."

"A will? Where are we getting to now?"

"It's complicated. Let's call it a love story and leave it at
that. A woman getting on in years who kills her lover because
he goes off with a young one."

"And what's become of them—the women?"

"The old one has only a few more months to live. It depends
on how much she drinks."

"How much she drinks?"

"Yes. Don't forget, it's not only a love story, but a drinking
story, too."

"You're right. It is complicated."

"More than you think. The old woman who killed her lover
will die in three or four months, or five, or six, with her legs
swollen and her feet in a basin of hot water."

"How do you know?"

"Look in your medical dictionary for how people end up
when they have dropsy."

"And the young one?"

"It's worse for her, because she loves the old one like a
mother. And besides that, she loves her pimp."

"Her what? You have a strange way of expressing yourself
today."

"Who will lose the twenty thousand francs at the races,"
went on Maigret imperturbably, eating all the time.

"What twenty thousand francs?"

"Never mind."

"I'm altogether out of my depth now."

"So am I. . . . Or, rather, I understand it all too well. I
was told to be tactful, and that's all. It's over and done with.
. . . A poor little love story with a miserable ending."

Then suddenly:

"There's no vegetable?"

"I wanted a cauliflower, but they weren't good."

And Maigret couldn't help thinking:

Jaja wanted love, but . . .